# When Dreams Abound

# When Dreams Abound

A Return to Chambers Lane

*Daniel Maldonado*

*This book is dedicated to my new-found younger sister, Lisa Maldonado, for being a source of silent strength when I was searching for answers. Since you entered my life, you've brought smiles and joy in ways unimaginable. Hope we get closer over the years.*

*I also would like to dedicate this book to my teachers, Robert Morris and George Kemper, as well as all of my teachers from Lynwood High School, Hosler Jr. High School, Ramona Elementary, and 10th Street Elementary School who encouraged me to look beyond myself, to become more than the sum of my parts, and to be a better person. Keep reaching beyond the stars!!!*

# Contents

Chapter One

# No Puerto Ricans

It was clear that the small house near the end of Chambers Lane sat on a lazy acre of land filled with various fruit trees. There was the large apricot tree that shaded the entire western face of the house. There was also the scrawny nectarine tree with only a few branches that barely produced two or three nectarines a year, but whose meager fruit was still juicy and delicious. Only one member of the Mendoza family was lucky enough to pick and eat the nectarines before the rest of the family had the opportunity to. Most of the time that was Jose Luis, the older brother, who would greedily eat the nectarines without any regard to anyone else. He was like that in every other way, especially when it came to food. Even his mother would claim that Jose Luis had a tapeworm or two because of the way he gorged food every day. Jose Luis would sneak into the refrigerator every night when everyone was asleep to eat the leftovers or eat the ingredients of the next day's meal. But this spring was different. Jose Luis did not eat the nectarines as he had eagerly anticipated. His younger brother, Daniel, had. Or at least that is what Jose Luis believed because Daniel had sat underneath the apricot tree every day dreamily contemplating something as he gazed towards the garden beyond. Between the garden and the apricot tree lay the nectarine tree and in Jose Luis' young, simple mind that was enough to indict Daniel. Little did Jose Luis know the real reason for Daniel's malaise that entire Spring. But it would not matter because Jose Luis could care less. Only the nectarines mattered to him and they were no more.

This evening, Jose Luis gazed out of his bedroom window. He could see Daniel sitting again under the apricot tree. Earlier that year, Daniel turned twelve. Twelve is a critical year. Daniel knew that next year he would be a teenager and that he would no longer be a child. He would be a man; not the way that other cultures view the transition into manhood and mark the occasion with religious or physical celebrations with family and friends and lots of food and gifts and rituals passed down through the ages. But Daniel would become a man the way that boys inherently view a change not only in their bodies, but also in their minds. The world looks different to a teenager. To a teenager, parents are now anathema. Teachers are still strange, but different in a way that makes life harder at times and hopeful at others. Grandparents are surprisingly cool because they are permissive and let their grandkids get into every sort of trouble so long as it makes them happy.

Daniel was leery of the changes that he would undergo as a teenager. Some of his older friends had changed and they no longer were friends with him. Now that his older friends attended the only middle school across town, they no longer saw Daniel on a daily basis. They made new friends with other students who had graduated from other elementary schools scattered around town. Daniel knew that the changes inside of him were inevitable. However, he wanted to savor his last year of innocence at least that was the way he saw it.

Even though Daniel planned to ensure that his simple life stayed the same, he had become estranged from his mother these past few months, invisible in ways that did not matter to him. At least, he convinced himself that it did not matter. His status as persona non grata gave him the free time to think and contemplate his future more than he usually did. He surprisingly thought of his upcoming independence, when he could make decisions on his own, when the need for adults to be a source of transportation to and from places was no longer required, when the future seemed brighter because every door was opened by thoughtful decisions strategically planned as if playing a board game whose outcome was already predetermined. He did his best thinking underneath the apricot tree. So he sat there every early evening like this evening, until the call for dinner was made and he had to join the rest of the family in a traditional repast. The other siblings would not bother him until then. His strange and often awkward demeanor was enough of a deterrent for his brother, Jose Luis, and his oldest sister, Maria. They stayed inside in their respective bedrooms watching television as usual. His younger sister, Sylvia, was oblivious to Daniel's absences. But Daniel did not mind. He was used to being a stranger in a strange family. He often joked that he was switched at birth at White Memorial Hospital. The other siblings were not amused.

This evening, Daniel had taken his writing book with him. The emerald cover was worn thin and a few pages were torn out after those times when he was displeased with the results. Some pages were dog-eared. But the current page where the pink, silk place marker was opened to was left blank. Not a single word or letter was even written that night. It was more of a silent comfort that distracted him. He was not disappointed with the lack of results. Nothing special had moved him that day. Instead, he had been gazing eerily into the distance past the garden as if nothing was within his field of view. The large, golden sunflowers that grew as tall as six feet did not even distract him. His contemplative attitude was engrossing, but he did not understand why it was so this evening. On occasion, he could hear the soft, but insistent calls of a blue-gray gnatcatcher as it hopped and sidled while foraging for insects and spiders in the garden. The gnatcatcher would lurk in the apricot tree just above Daniel's head awaiting more prey. Even this, Daniel would ignore.

What Daniel could not ignore was the inescapable aroma of the evening's meal that his mother, Lucia Maria Mendoza, was cooking because it would waft outside and engulf his senses. He could smell the faint peppery and nutty tones of the orange-red annatto seeds that were harvested from an achiote tree. His mother stirred the fragrant seeds into the olive oil along with the chopped onions and garlic. He could hear the searing of the salt pork and small pieces of ham. Then she would add the diced cubanelle peppers, carrots, tomatoes, and Spanish olives that formed the foundation of the evening's meal. Having watched his mother cook this Puerto Rican dish many times, Daniel knew that she would soon season the ingredients with adobo and cumin and also include a bay leaf or two so that they would add a slight floral scent as well as a pungent and sharp, bitter taste to the dish. Daniel sensed that his mother was making pollo guisado. He knew that she would also make some white rice in the large, metallic caldero that she cooked in practically every evening. The chicken stew, as it is vernacularly referred to, would be served on top of the rice and consumed quickly by the family. Even Daniel was eager to consume it.

"Dinner's ready," Lucia yelled so that the kids could hear. She knew that Daniel was typically outside. So this evening, like most evenings in the Spring of 1977, she would yell louder so that Daniel could hear her and she did not have to go outside herself to fetch him or send one of the other children to do so.

This evening, Daniel was reluctant to come inside and deal with any of the family drama. But the grumblings of his stomach were too irresistible, so he relented. He arose from sitting on the grass lawn and walked slowly back to the front porch. As he was about to open the front door, he heard his mother say, "Wipe your feet on the doormat before you come in!! I don't want you tracking dirt inside."

4

Daniel begrudgingly complied, but he was already used to this daily ritual. He looked down towards the worn, brown carpet that festooned the joint living room/dining room area where the family would eat their meals. He wondered to himself, "Why bother? It's old, dilapidated carpet anyway," but he dared not upset his mother. Daniel knew that his father would arrive shortly and that his mother did not want anything to disturb his father after a long day's work. So Daniel complied and proceeded quietly to the dining room table.

Seated already was Jose Luis on the far right chair closer to where he knew that his mother would place the food because it was closest to the kitchen. He was eager as always to eat any meal. Jose Luis looked stupidly towards Daniel as he walked into the house. Jose Luis was holding back a laugh that his grinning face easily betrayed. He knew that his mother would backhand him if he made his typical flippant comment so he refrained from doing so. Jose Luis did not want to be sent to his room without dinner. He was already thirteen and was one year older than Daniel. But unlike Daniel, Jose Luis was unwilling to grow up. He spent most of his free time outside of school with neighborhood kids several years his junior. These kids were typically nine or ten years old. Jose Luis felt like the leader of his "gang." His mother frowned in disappointment of her son's shenanigans with whom she described as fellow hooligans. In Lucia's mind, her oldest son's actions belittled the family's reputation in the community.

To Jose Luis's left was Sylvia. She was seven years younger than Daniel. The age difference had an impact on their relationship. Sylvia was rambunctious with her many kindergarten friends at school, but she never really played with her own siblings. They wanted very little to do with her, mainly because she was the youngest and their mother's favorite. Daniel sat next to her at the table. He ignored her as well as his salty brother and looked straight ahead towards the hallway, waiting for the food to be served.

"Maria!!! When are you coming to the kitchen?" her mother inquired. "We are waiting for you." Lucia carried two bowls full of the pollo guisado, one in each hand, and walked toward the dining room table. She placed one in front of Jose Luis and the other she placed in front of Sylvia. "Junior, bring the caldero of rice to the table." He ignored her and grabbed a spoon to start feeding himself. Lucia grabbed his left ear and roughly pulled his face toward her. "I said get the rice. Boy, you heard me. Don't make me regret feeding you first!"

Jose Luis reluctantly rose from the table with a sour look and listlessly walked to the kitchen. As he was returning with the pot of rice, Maria entered from the hallway. Her face was gleaming with excitement. "Roberto asked me to the dance!!"

"You know mom's not going to let you go," Jose Luis exclaimed while almost dropping the caldero onto the dining room floor.

"Ay Dios mio. Be careful. You're gonna drop it." Lucia walked quickly toward Jose Luis to ensure that he did not. When the rice was safely on the table, she turned towards Maria and said, "Your father doesn't want you going out and dating anyone until you are sixteen. You know that Maria. If I had my way, it wouldn't be until you were eighteen. You know how I feel about boys your age."

"I'm not going to wait another two years before I start dating. I will miss the prom and homecoming and many dances in between," Maria retorted.

"You're never going to any of those things so give it up," Jose Luis added. Daniel sat quietly listening. Because Jose Luis was doing a surprisingly great job, Daniel did not feel the need to interject. Besides, Maria would only use it against him later if he did. Even if Daniel said nothing, Maria would also use that against him for not sticking up for her. Jose Luis never cared about any retribution Maria could exact. So long as he had his gang, he was fine.

Just then, the front door opened. A swankily dressed man of thirty-five years old walked into the house with his briefcase in his hand. He placed his outer coat on the sofa on the opposite side of the living room and took his Stetson hat off, leaving the briefcase alongside the sofa near the entrance of the hallway. The room was eerily quiet during this ritual. All eyes were on Jose Luis Mendoza, Senior until he sat down at the head of the table furthest from the kitchen. Until then, no one said a word. Not even the smart-mouthed older son.

"Dinner smells delicious. What's this about a prom?" he asked. Maria was loathed to respond knowing that it may upset both of her parents.

"It's nothing," Lucia replied.

"I heard you guys talking about it right before I came in." Mr. Mendoza tucked his napkin on his lap and grabbed one of the bowls from the table so that he could serve himself some pollo guisado. Lucia moved the caldero of rice closer to him. He did not like to be served. Once he finished serving himself, Lucia served Daniel and Maria and then herself.

"How was your day?" Lucia asked. He took this question as a sign that his wife did not want to talk about the prom and other events that he had just inquired about in front of the children. So he let the matter go. He knew that Lucia would bring it up herself shortly after the children went to bed and they were alone.

Jose Luis, Senior proceeded to tell his wife and the rest of the family about the long day at work, his promotion to general manager, and the accompanying raise. Unbeknownst to him, his supervisor, Avery Smith, had placed his name in consideration for promotion. Jose had worked there for nearly a decade. He had given up on any advancement until Avery was hired two years ago. Lucia had prayed for this moment and was also encouraged when Jose's former supervisor was fired and the New

Englander Smith took his place. She was overjoyed when she heard the news of the promotion. The entire family was.

Maria dreamed of money for a prom dress. Jose Luis, Junior contemplated finally getting a remote control car so that he could play in the nearby empty field with the other members of his gang. Sylvia was clueless. But in reality, she always received everything that she wanted and the news would not truly alter her good fortune. Lucia wanted the fur coat on sale at the recently opened Montgomery Wards on the other side of town. She had seen the fur coat when she visited her bridge club teammate, Ophelia Cummings, on the other side of town. Daniel wondered how the news would affect him, but nothing came to mind.

The entire house was alight with the news until Mr. Mendoza turned to Daniel and said, "We can finally pay for your college tuition. I have high hopes for you, Daniel. You will attend a great college; the best that money can buy. I was talking to Avery, Mr. Smith, and he suggested that you should go to UCLA. It's one of the highest ranking public schools in the country and is ranked in the top 20 in the entire world. The best thing is that it's here in Los Angeles. You can live here with us and you don't have to go to some Ivy League school back east and get into huge debt. We can all support you in your endeavors. I'll take you to the campus someday soon so you can see for yourself. I'll take all of you."

Mr. Mendoza smiled. He was very proud of himself and very proud that he had plans for his younger son who was the only one in the family to show any interest in higher education and going to college. Mrs. Mendoza always discouraged her husband from openly encouraging Daniel to go to college especially in front of the other children who had no such aspirations. She worried that they would get the impression that somehow their father did not care for them as much because of it. Her husband rejected this as nonsense and hoped that his encouragement would positively affect the other children. He had not yet seen the fruits of these attempts, but there was still some time. There were four more years before his eldest child, Maria, would graduate from high school. Mr. Mendoza was less hopeful towards his eldest son and had lowered his expectations. Daniel, on the other hand, resented these overt comments because the other siblings would openly ridicule him. That was the last thing Daniel needed given his own eccentric personality. Although Daniel could care less for their approval, the emotional derisions were unbearable at times. So Daniel did not respond to his father latest comments, but only listened attentively with tepid excitement.

As the pre-dinner conversation began to wind down, they all waited for Mr. Mendoza to stop talking and to bless their food so that they could all eat. He grabbed his wife's hand with his left hand and clasped Daniel's with his right hand. Mrs. Mendoza also grabbed Maria's hand. The others also held hands for the evening's prayer before dinner and they all bowed their heads and closed their eyes. When Mr. Mendoza finished praying, Daniel lifted his head and opened his eyes only to find that he was in fact not sitting at the dining room table, but was sitting alone on the edge of his bed watching television. A cold plate of rice and beans was on his lap and a fork in his hand. It was the typical place where Daniel ate dinner in the evenings. He could hear Maria in her own bedroom eating dinner and Sylvia in her room as well. Jose Luis had apparently already eaten because his plate sat empty on the bedroom floor. He was taking a nap on the adjacent bed next to Daniel.

As Daniel continued eating his dinner, the television began to loudly blare out "I don't want any Puerto Ricans living in this house." Daniel looked up from his plate and turned to look at the screen. It was another episode of Sanford and Son, one of Daniel's favorite shows. He watched the show in his room whenever it came on when he ate dinner. The main character,

Fred Sanford, a cantankerousness older black man whose gray hair and scruffy gray beard were distinguishing, continued to cup both hands around his mouth as he repeatedly shouted at the top of his lungs that he did not want any Puerto Ricans living in his house. Daniel had seen this episode several times before. Daniel sat upright on his bed stupefied that his recent thoughts of a loving family happily eating together were only a figment of his imagination.

Chapter Two

# A Card is Just a Card

Irma Sanchez had been Daniel's fourth grade teacher when he had attended Ramona Elementary School before the Mendoza family moved to Chambers Lane. The school was located in West Hollywood on Santa Monica Boulevard, east of the 101 freeway. At that time, the Mendoza family lived on Serrano Avenue. Daniel and his older siblings would walk every school day the several miles from their home towards Western Avenue and then east along Santa Monica to get to school. Daniel was always eager to get to class. He typically walked first, far ahead of the other siblings. His dark brown, rectangular backpack would be overflowing with books. Daniel would have to pull both straps along his chest downwards; otherwise the backpack would be too heavy for his small frame and he would be pulled backwards towards the ground. Jose Luis would often trail far behind at the end of the pack with nothing in hand, not even a pencil. Jose Luis would walk aimlessness and laugh and giggle as Daniel struggled ahead of him. Maria had some books in her hand as she walked. Typically, one or two of Maria's books had a brown paper bag book cover. Maria had drawn pictures on the book covers of characters that she liked. The newest was an unsophisticated, crayon drawing of Laura Ingalls; Maria's latest fascination. Maria was usually a few yards behind Daniel.

The three continued walking on Santa Monica until they crossed Normandie Avenue. Once they reached Normandie, then they would need to enter the underground, pedestrian tunnel that crossed Santa Monica. It was still open to the public then. But the dark, dank tunnel was scary. So they always waited for each other at the southern entrance before they all entered together. They hurriedly walked or sometimes ran across the tunnel and up the stairs to the sidewalk where they would finally feel safe again. Months before they eventually moved to Chambers Lane, this underground tunnel, like most, similar tunnels in the Los Angeles basin, had been fenced in and closed off to prevent crime. At that point, the siblings would just cross the vast and heavily, trafficked Santa Monica Boulevard after waiting a long time for a green light.

But on typical mornings like today, once the three reached the surface of the pedestrian tunnel, they then continued walking along the northern side of Santa Monica until they reached the next street, Mariposa Avenue. Although the main entrance of Ramona Elementary was the double doors of the historic main building on Mariposa, students were not allowed to enter them. Only teachers and administrators were allowed to enter the school by the main doors. Students were only allowed to use the main door when they were accompanied by a parent. Because Mrs. Mendoza never accompanied her children to school, they always walked alone. So the three siblings would have to only walk the short distance up Mariposa until they reached the first gate entrance of the chain-linked fence that surrounded the entire school. They would walk west towards the auditorium, but then head north to the side entrance that lead to the cafeteria where they would stand in line to obtain that morning's breakfast.

By the time they reached the cafeteria, they were slightly sweaty. They would cool down while waiting in line for about ten or fifteen minutes before they were finally allowed to enter the cafeteria. Once entering they would be given could a tray so that the cafeteria women, who usually volunteered their time, could serve them breakfast. Most of the time it was pancakes or waffles. But this morning, it was scrambled eggs with a biscuit and two strips of bacon and a triangular-shaped container with orange juice. All of the school kids always loved this seemingly fresh orange juice. The kids would blow the plastic wrap around their straw onto their neighbors. It was somewhat of an informal school tradition that everyone enjoyed. Unlikely, the formal school tradition that every student dreaded every morning while eating breakfast at the cafeteria. Inevitably, the school principle, Ms. Angela Bullocks, would ominously enter the cafeteria with a Cruella DeVille-esque aura that would drain the life out of each student. Even the workers were afraid of her. She would hold a black and tan, Norwich terrier with a harsh, wiry coat that she would gently stroke as she requested silence from everyone inside. The entire group quickly complied as it awaited her typically short words of encouragement of all the students. Once she left the cafeteria each morning, none of the students ever saw Ms. Bullocks again throughout the day except those naughty children who were sent to her office for misbehaving.

The cafeteria would again fill with boisterous laughter and chatter once Ms. Bullocks left. Daniel usually sat alone, away from his other siblings, so he was still quiet when the principal left the room. This morning, he was readying himself for the day's lesson. He looked around the cafeteria. Jose Luis would typically eat his breakfast outside and was not in sight when Daniel's eyes circumnavigated the room. Maria was with the group of sixth-grade girls that she typically hung out with. Daniel was looking for his deskmate, Alfredo Barraza. They both shared the same two-person lift lid school desk with its faux oak desktop made out of high-pressure laminate fiberboard and a steel frame with chrome legs.

On the first day of school, each student was asked by Ms. Sanchez to pair up and pick a desk partner. Daniel was the odd man out and had no partner. He was happy that he did not have to share his desk with anyone. Daniel had to share his room and almost everything else he owned with his older brother, Jose Luis. Jose Luis seemed to destroy practically everything he touched or used and was ambivalent about anything of Daniel's that he destroyed. Having no partner at school was a welcomed change. However, about a half hour after the students paired up and Daniel had staked out his own desk, Alfredo entered the classroom late. Unfortunately for Alfredo, his parents drove him to school that day and they escorted him up the main stairs through the main doors of the main entrance of the school. Ms. Bullocks was happy to greet one of the few parents to actually come to the school. She invited Alfredo's parents to her office so that she can give them her usual spiel about school life at Ramona Elementary. Alfredo dreaded it, but he was excused for being thirty minutes late.

When he entered Ms. Sanchez's class, she was pleasantly surprised. As a sign of her happiness, Ms. Sanchez would typically lift her black cat eyeglasses from her nose and let them hang with the beaded eyeglass chain that clipped on to them. She could look directly at the person that she was talking to when she did this. As Ms. Sanchez lifted her glasses to look at Alfredo, her eyeglass chain caught on her short hair that had steep-angled layers cut all around the sides and back, which created a triangular shape that was longer on top. The back of Ms. Sanchez's hair was heavily-layered. This layering was the inadvertent culprit that caused the eyeglass chain to get caught. Luckily, Ms Sanchez easily recovered and quickly loosened the chain from her hair as if she had experienced this before. All of the students were unaware, even Alfredo. She asked Alfredo to introduce himself and he willingly compiled. Because Daniel was the only unpaired student, Ms. Sanchez assigned Alfredo as his deskmate. Daniel had to clear off the left side of the desk with his things so that Alfredo would have a place to put his pencils and pencil sharpener, rulers, erasers, and other supplies that he brought with him. Alfredo did not have a pencil holder. Daniel decided to give Alfredo his own spare, orange Fred Flintstone pencil holder that he got as a prize inside the Fruity Pebbles cereal box. Daniel also gave him a blue Dino coin purse so that Alfredo could store his milk money inside. Alfredo placed the pencil holder on the top left of the desk and put the coin purse in his pocket. After that, the two were good friends.

So Daniel was surprised when he could not locate Alfredo in the cafeteria that morning. It was early June 1974. Daniel knew that Alfredo's family had plans for the summer to visit Aguascalientes in north-central Mexico. Alfredo's parents wanted to visit his ailing grandmother who lived near the Zacatecas border. Daniel realized that it was too early for Alfredo's family to leave already because school was still in session. Surely, they would want Alfredo to finish out the semester before traveling to Mexico. Daniel became worried that Alfredo's grandmother had taken a turn for the worse. He was afraid that he would lose his deskmate for the remainder of the school year, which did not have too many days left. Even still, Daniel and Alfredo were close and any time together, even if only a few day, would be welcomed and cherished.

Once Alfredo entered the cafeteria from the hallway, Daniel's concerns were alleviated. The two met up and eventually walked back to the hallway, walked up the circular stairwell to the second floor, and then into Ms. Sanchez's classroom. As fourth graders, they were assigned to her class all day and did not have to switch rooms for each period like the sixth graders did. Ms. Sanchez taught them every subject. This morning was different. After taking attendance, Ms. Sanchez did not start with the instructions for the first morning's assignment, which was English. Instead, she wheeled over a table full of construction paper, markers, crayons, watercolor pan sets, and brushes to the front of the classroom. All of the students were surprised.

"Okay class, settle down. We are not going to continue with today's reading of 'Tales of a Fourth Grade Nothing.'" The class had just started reading the book early that week, which had recently been written by Judy Blume only a few years earlier. "I know some of you are going to be disappointed." Ms. Sanchez could see Daniel in the corner of her eye. He was somewhat dejected. "But I promise you that this will be a fun assignment and that you will like it. In a few days, it will be Father's Day. We always do something special for Mother's Day. But this year, I want to be fair and do something for Father's Day. I'm sure your fathers like getting the ties or belts or other things that you guys give them. But this year, I thought that your fathers would like a personal card from each one of you. So you're welcome to use any of the supplies on this table to create a Father's Day card. You can paint, draw, or do whatever you want to the card. Just make sure you return any unused supplies and clean up your desk before this period ends."

Ms. Sanchez sat down and watched her students walk to the table to pick up supplies. Daniel and Alfredo were furthest from the table so they were the last in line. Ms. Sanchez had purchased plenty of supplies so being last did not matter. Both Alfredo and Daniel had every option available to make a card. Daniel decided to pick some of each type of supplies provided and walked back to his seat. Alfredo was only moments ahead of him and sat down first. Daniel watched as Alfredo used his scissors to cut down the blue construction paper to a ten-inch by six-inch rectangle. He proceeded to decorate the card. As he did so, Daniel looked around the classroom and saw that the other kids are busy cutting and drawing on their construction paper for their cards. Daniel continued to look around the room wondering what the other kids were writing. He began fiddling with the construction paper that he selected and trimmed it down as well.

After cutting the paper to the size of a Hallmark card, Daniel stopped and looked at the empty paper. He began wondering what to write and had a befuddled look on his face. He stood still for a moment, but then started fiddling with the black marker in his hand. He twirled it endlessly and sometimes pounding one end on the desktop or putting it in his mouth and taking the cap off and on, and off and on.

From across the room, Ms. Sanchez could see the bewildering look on Daniel's face. She walked over to his desk, placed her arm around his shoulder and asked, "Is everything okay, Daniel?"

Daniel stumbled in his response to Ms. Sanchez, but he thought to himself that he does not know what is a father. "No. Everything is okay. I'm just trying to figure out something special to write," Daniel finally responded.

Ms. Sanchez smiled. "Okay. Let me know if you need anything." She quietly walked back to the front of the classroom and continued monitoring the other students.

Daniel looked over to his left to see what Alfredo was writing, but his right arm was blocking the view. Since Daniel was very young, his mother had always been a single mom. He was too young to understand that she divorced his father when Daniel was only a year old. He had no memory of his father. There were no pictures of his father in the family home that his mother rented. Daniel's mother never spoke of their father or his father's family. The Mendoza family certainly never celebrated Father's Day. Daniel had not even heard of the holiday until Ms. Sanchez mentioned it that day. Unbeknownst to Daniel, his father's family no longer lived in the Los Angeles area. Daniel's mother no longer visited them after the divorce. Nor did his father's family babysit Daniel and his siblings when his mother needed a break or was ill.

The only person Lucia Mendoza could truly rely upon was her sister, Belen. Daniel's Aunt, Belen, was also divorced. She got divorced around the same time that Daniel's mother did. When Lucia spent time with Belen, there were also no men in her house. Neither were there any pictures of a happy marriage. Although Daniel was nine years old at this time, he had not learned about the birds and the bees. His mother never spoke of that topic. When Daniel was in the fourth grade, schools only provided sex education to girls and only when they were in the sixth grade because many girls would begin their menstrual cycle around that age. Boys had to wait to be taught about the birds and bees until they were in the tenth grade if their parents never broached the topic. Daniel did not know that it took a man and a woman to create a baby. In fact, he never even thought about how he came into existence. This assignment was perplexing to him. He was normally the top student in his class, every class, but this issue had evaded him all these years.

After a while, Daniel knew that he had to write something on the card and decorate it. He did not want to fail this assignment. It would be the first time he would have failed an assignment. He knew that his mother would not be pleased if he failed. His anxiety increased. He thought and thought, but the more he thought, the more he was stuck. Until finally, he decided to write what he was thinking:

I don't know who you are, what you are, or what you should mean to me. I do know that I'm supposed to celebrate you today.

Daniel was not truly happy with it. He did not know whether it would be enough to get a high enough grade to pass the assignment. He only hoped that Ms. Sanchez would give him credit for his honesty and understanding. Daniel knew that was the best that he could do for this assignment. So he tried not to be too disappointed in himself even if he was. He wondered why Ms. Sanchez would even have such an assignment. Could there be other boys in the class like him who had no fathers? Did Ms. Sanchez know that? Should she have known that about

Daniel? He never mentioned it to her. He had no idea that he even needed to mention it to her before today. Did boys even have fathers? Daniel had never gone to Alfredo's house. They only saw each other at school. Daniel had never gone to any of his friend's house and they never came to his. He did not even know if Alfredo had a father. Daniel never saw Alfredo's parents. He just assumed that Alfredo only had a mother just like Daniel did.

"Surely, Ms. Sanchez will understand," he thought to himself.

Daniel was relieved when the period ended and Ms. Sanchez never collected the cards. She did not grade the assignment. She just told everyone to save the card and give it to their father on Father's Day. Daniel did not even know what day that was. For the rest of the day, Daniel was still disturbed. He knew that he created a Father's Day card, but that he had no one to give the card to. As he walked home with his siblings, this time Daniel walked slowly home rather than the quick pace that he normally would walk. He normally walked fast because he wanted to get home quickly and start his homework. But today, Daniel walked so slowly that even Jose Luis was ahead of him. This time Daniel trailed the other siblings. Despite the obvious signs, Jose Luis and Maria did not realize that something was wrong with Daniel and that something was bothering him. If they did, Daniel could not see any concerns from his siblings.

As Daniel was walking home on Santa Monica Boulevard, he realized that Jose Luiz and Maria were so far ahead of him that they could not see him. He continued to unblithely walk without a purpose. When he reached the corner of Hobart Boulevard, Daniel saw a trashcan on the sidewalk near the liquor store. He walked fast-paced until he reached the trashcan and then he stopped. Daniel looked ahead to see if Jose Luis and Maria could see him. He did not see them in the distance. Daniel then looked around both sides of the street to see if he could recognize any students from Ramona Elementary School. His heart palpitated quickly when he realized that no one was around. He took off his backpack, unzipped it, took out the card, ripped it up and threw it in the trashcan.

Daniel stood quietly, hovering over the trashcan for a few minutes until he finally got the nerve to leave and walk the rest of the way home alone. Later that evening, Daniel contemplated asking his mother what is a father, but he decided against it.

Chapter Three

# Eyes of a Different Color

The entire background was set to light gray, but the two-dimensional walls delineating the combat playing field were a yellow-green more reminiscent of aged guacamole. All of the intermittent walls scattered throughout the field formed somewhat of a simple maze that the players could hide behind or bounce their guided or straight missiles against. The walls were also the same puky guacamole color that was common in multi-directional shooter games that came with the Atari 2600 console. Gabriel had received the Atari console as a Christmas gift the winter of 1978. Gabriel skillfully maneuvered his reddish tank around the L-shaped structure and fired towards the burgundy-ish tank. He scored a hit just before the time ran out, winning the game. His smirky smile said it all. He was happy to still be the reigning champion of the Tank game, even if it was only just his other three younger brothers who he remained victorious over. Gabriel had never played with anyone else before, not even with the other boys who lived in his immediate neighborhood.

"That's not fair. You cheated. You always cheat!" His youngest brother Rigoberto exclaimed. "I'm going to tell mom." He started to get up to walk out the Gabriel's bedroom.

"Go ahead. She's not here." Gabriel could not hold back his laugh. He knew that their mother would be gone the entire weekend and that he and his brothers would be stuck home alone with no way to go anywhere. "What did I tell you, Daniel? He's a sore loser. That's why I didn't want to play him in the first place. You want to play?"

"Sure. I'll try. I've never played this game before."

Two years earlier, Daniel's mother had bought a black and white television set for his older sister Maria. His mother also bought one for Daniel and his brother, Jose Luis, to share. Sylvia also had her own television set. But Daniel's mother never bought them any consoles to play any video games. She did not want to waste any money on such nonsense. At least, that is what she told her children whenever they asked for one. But they suspected that the real reason why she refused to buy a console was because, when she would occasionally take them to the Sears on Santa Monica Boulevard west of Western Avenue when they lived on Serrano, she always lost at Pong. They suspected that she hated losing and did not want to have to endure that in her own home; certainly not on a daily basis. So Daniel and Jose Luis would have to be content walking the two blocks from their home on Chambers Lane to Wright Road so that they could at least play pinball at Jo Jo's cafe. They would play whenever they had a spare quarter or two. But that was becoming tedious and boring. They both wanted a new challenge.

Daniel had no idea that his new friend, Gabriel Ramirez, who he recently meet at Hosler Junior High School, had a console at his house. They met for the first time in Mr. Lucas's science class during their fourth period on the first day of the seventh grade class. Daniel sat up front like he normally did and shortly thereafter Gabriel sat in the chair next to him. When Mr. Lucas asked the class a question, both Daniel and Gabriel would be the only ones who raised their hands. They would fight to be the first one to answer. They became quick friends even though they could not explain why or exactly when it happened. After a few weeks of school, once Gabriel's mother decided to spend the weekend in Tijuana, Gabriel invited Daniel to spend the night at his house. Daniel was reluctant to accept because his mother had never let any of her children spend the night at one of their friend's house. He decided to take a chance and ask anyway. The worst that would happen was that his mother would say "No." He was surprised that she actually said "yes." Daniel anxiously awaited that upcoming Friday. He was so excited that he forgot to pack. Daniel did not mind having any spare clothes to wear so long as he got a chance to get away and enjoy Gabriel and his three brothers.

Now, Daniel had a chance to play some of Gabriel's Atari games. Gabriel let Daniel play the red tank during the Combat game. Daniel struggled with the controller and was clumsy with it. In no time, Gabriel maneuvered his tank behind Daniel's red tank so that Gabriel's cannon was inserted into the rear cutout of Daniel's tank. Once in this position, Gabriel then rotated his tank causing a collision that sent Daniel's tank into a wild jump, making it leave the edge of the right side of the television screen and then enter the left side. Daniel was fascinated.

"Whoa! How did you do that?" Daniel exclaimed.

"Skill. Daniel. Skill." Gabriel laughed. He could not help himself. The two were always competitive, but this was the first area where Gabriel had a significant advantage. Gabriel was going to relish it for as long as he could.

When the game was over, Gabriel allowed his youngest brother, Rigoberto, and his other brother, Francisco, to play the bi-plane version of the video game. While they were doing so, Gabriel asked Daniel to follow him into the kitchen so that they could get a cold glass of Cactus Cooler. It was Gabriel's favorite soda.

"Here, try some." After pouring some soda for himself, Gabriel gave Daniel a glass of soda. "I'm glad that my mom's not here. I took some of the money she left us to buy my favorite drink at Lion's King. My brothers like it too. They are tired of the cheap sodas that my mom buys from TJ. Sure, they come in a nice glass bottle, but the cane sugar gives it a different taste. I don't like it. I'm a fructose man myself." Gabriel grinned excitedly.

Daniel was confused, but did not bother to ask for an explanation. He knew that it did not matter in the end. Both boys sat at the kitchen table so that they could continue their conversation and continued to drink their refreshments.

"I like it. It has a refreshing taste," Daniel said after taking a few gulps of his drink. Gabriel was pleased that his new best friend also loved his favorite drink. But Gabriel knew that Daniel would like Cactus Cooler because the two boys had so many things in common. "Is that why your mom's in TJ? To buy soda?" Daniel asked.

"Soda. Cheap meats. My mom goes grocery shopping in TJ every month."

"Why?" Daniel asked.

Daniel remembered going to Tijuana several years earlier for Easter. He had no idea why his mother wanted to do that. They spent most of the day window shopping along Avenida Revolucion in the heart of Tijuana Daniel pictured the marionette of a Mexican male that his mom bought him and his brother, Jose Luis. The puppet wore red, cotton pants with a simulated white guayabera shirt. The shirts worn by the puppet did not have the fancy embroidery that real guayabera shirts that are traditionally worn have. It also had a small straw hat to apparently give it an authentic feel to tourists who would unwittingly purchase them as souvenirs. The hands and face were made of paper mache; the bright brown painted face with rosy red cheeks was fading and chipping slightly. Daniel did not mind because he could make the wooden feet dance and stomp loudly by manipulating the marionette with the stings. Having spent all day walking and entering the various shops, Daniel considered it a tourist trap with nothing really exciting to buy or do. The only thing that he enjoyed besides the flavorful, authentic Mexican food, was the time his mother relented and agreed to let a man take a picture of her children on a mule that was painted like a zebra hauling a wagon. The kids mistakenly believed that it was an actually zebra from the wild, but they were later dispossessed of that notion once they were back in the States. The black and white photo had Maria sitting on the faux zebra while Daniel and Jose Luis sat behind her on the wagon. Each child was wearing their Sunday best along with an embroidered sombrero that the photographer gave them to wear, which when combined formed the expressive statement: "I love You. Kiss Me, Mexico." What tourist would not love such an experience? Given the rest of his dull experience with Tijuana, Daniel was surprised that Gabriel's mother, Lupe Zepeda, would buy her groceries there. He never really wanted to return and wondered why anyone would because the stores sold the same useless trinkets as ever other stores, like the marionette given to Daniel and his siblings, or Mexican rugs, ponchos, or even Snoopy ceramics.

"Because everything is so cheap there compared to grocery stores here. It's cheaper than Lion's King. It's so cheap that mom even goes to TJ for her dental work. She was just there two months ago to see the dentist," Gabriel explained.

"Dental work? Really? Does she trust a Mexican dentist?"

"I don't trust Mexican doctors myself. But my mom does. She was born in Tijuana. She's always going there to visit her family and save money. She has great insurance with GM so I don't know why she even needs to go to any doctors in TJ." Gabriel's voice betrayed his frustration.

Ms. Zepeda had worked for the General Motors plant in Van Nuys in San Fernando Valley since she was twenty years old. She was always pro-American when it came to her cars, but pro-Mexican when it came to everything else. Her latest and newest car was a 1978 burgundy Buick Regal. She always bought her cars from GM because she received the employee price. The boys loved the hefty V-6 engine and the luxury suspension made for a softer ride than the last GM car that she purchased. They hated the coupe design because it meant that Gabriel sat in the front passenger seat because he was the oldest son. Gabriel refused to budge from the passenger seat to let his brothers in once he was seated. He did not believe that he should inconvenience himself because the other boys were always late. So they had to crawl into the rear seat by folding the driver's vinyl, bucket seat forward. Ms. Zepeda would get annoyed every time one of her sons was finally ready, which was never at the same time forcing Ms. Zepeda to get up from her seat ever five minutes or so. The annoyance meant that there was inevitably a fight every time the family had to go somewhere. That was why Ms. Zepeda went to Tijuana with her boyfriend, Julio, without her children. She wanted to avoid any aggravation and enjoy the weekend by herself.

Gabriel, however, did not like going to Mexico; not because of the frustration that occurred every time the family loaded into the car, but because it reminded him of an inescapable abnormality that was obvious to anyone who looked at Gabriel even if he did not remove his large, Coke-bottle glasses from his face. Gabriel's left eye was vibrantly, light blue, but his eye wandered inward or outward all the time. It was a lazy eye, while his right eye was normal and a deep, dark brown. Daniel had always assumed that it was a genetic defect. He never asked Gabriel about his eye at any time during the short time that they knew each other and he considered it rude to bring it up. He figured that Gabriel would do so once he felt comfortable. So Daniel was surprised to hear that Gabriel's distrust of Mexican doctors (Gabriel being Mexican himself) had to do with his left eye.

Gabriel explained that, when his mother was pregnant with him, she did not want to pay her insurance deductible so she never saw an American doctor that was part of GM's robust, Cadillac network plan. Instead, she would drive two hours past San Diego, cross the San Ysidro border crossing into Tijuana, and then drive to Dr. Lopez's clinic near Rosarito beach. She made this trip monthly during her pregnancy because she had decided that she wanted a Mexican doctor to deliver her first baby. During delivery, Dr. Lopez tried to speed up the delivery process by trying to extract Gabriel using obstetrical forceps, causing damage to his left eye. When Gabriel was older, he suspected that Dr. Lopez was either drunk during the delivery or he was anxious to get his final payment.

"I can't believe that she risked injuring me to save a couple of bucks." Gabriel put down his half-empty glass of Cactus Cooler and slowly twirled the top of the glass with his hands while staring deeply into it. He stopped twirling the glass and stomped it slightly on the table. "She doesn't know how that ruined my life!! I can't really see out of my left eye. I have to wear these stupid glasses. No girls are attracted to me because of my lazy eye so I'll never have a girlfriend. I want nothing to do with her and her cheap trips to TJ to save money." The exasperation in Gabriel's voice was telling.

Surprisingly, Daniel had not realized that Gabriel had this underlying source of anger and frustration. In the few weeks that Daniel knew Gabriel, in addition to being intelligent and an overachiever, Gabriel was also the class clown in every junior high school class that he and Daniel had together. This jovial attitude oftentimes got Gabriel into trouble with his teachers, but he always had a way of talking himself out of detention or being sent to the principal's office. Daniel admired him for that. Hearing the story of Gabriel's disdain towards his mother and his abnormality now made Daniel feel sympathetic towards him. But he knew that Gabriel did not want his sympathy, just his understanding. So Daniel tried to avoid giving that appearance. Surely Gabriel needed some time to finally deal with his feeling so that he would be in a better place and reconcile with his mother.

"Well, if you don't like living here with your mom, why don't you move in with your dad?" Daniel had never met Gabriel's father, but would on occasion hear Ms. Zepeda mention him. Daniel had not realized that he brought up another sore subject that Gabriel did not really like to discuss. Discussions of Gabriel's father would bring up bad memories. But Gabriel decided that he really liked Daniel's friendship and wanted to be better friends. Besides, he had just disclosed a secret to Daniel that he had never told anyone else. What would it matter if Gabriel discussed his father? It was not like any of it was not obvious to the casual observer of his family dynamics.

"I know you will understand, Daniel. At least, I hope you do."

Gabriel explained that his parents met while they both worked at General Motors. They both worked the second shift from four p.m. to midnight. But after they fell in love, got married, and had children, Gabriel's mother was assigned to the third shift from midnight to eight a.m. His father, Manuel Zepeda, did not want his mother working the third shift. Not only did Mr. Zepeda not want to sleep alone at night without the comfort of his wife, but he also did not want to have to take care of his children by himself. That was a woman's job according to Mr. Zepeda. Mrs. Zepeda argued that the third shift allowed her to receive an extra dollar per hour shift differential that the family really needed now that there were five mouths to feed. She did not heed her husband's desire and took the position without his consent. He was certainly displeased, but believed that after a few months his wife would want to switch back to the second shift. Mr. Zepeda believed that the new schedule would wear his wife out physically. Little did Mr. Zepeda know that there were advantages to his wife working the third shift that outweighed any exhaustion issues that she ultimately had. Mostly, she could sleep during the day when the kids were off to school and be awake when they came home from school to cook them dinner. She could also help them with their homework or just be with her children in the evenings. When she worked the second shift, she was gone when her children got home and they were already in bed when her shift finished. Mrs. Zepeda rarely saw her sons except during the weekends when she worked the second shift. After the shift change, she saw them all the time. Mr. Zepeda, however, did not.

When the months working the second shift turned into years, Mr. Zepeda became resentful and more distant from his wife. He sought comfort in the arms of a younger, female co-worker. When Mrs. Zepeda eventually found out, she wanted nothing to do with him and told him to leave the house and never come back. Mr. Zepeda thought this was just her initial reaction, but that she would be more forgiving once she realized her own role in the marriage's demise for switching to the third shift and defying her husband. The forgiveness, however, was not forthcoming. Instead, Mrs. Zepeda hired a Mexican lawyer in Tijuana and filed for divorce.

"It's her fault," Gabriel added. "She married a traditional Mexican man and refused to live like a traditional wife or listen to him. What husband wants to be the provider and take care of his kids while his wife in on the streets. I don't blame him. To make matters worse, my mom wouldn't let my dad see us. She was too proud and wanted to punish him for what he did. I may see him maybe once a year. He tried to reconcile with her, but she would have none of it. I told her that we needed our father back, especially Rigoberto because he is the youngest, and that she should take him back. Did she listen to me? No. Pendejo is what she called me. Pendejo!!! I can't believe my own mother called me that. She is the pendejo for letting him go. He made good money and always took care of us. Now she is out with her lazy boyfriend who doesn't even have a job, who just does what she says, and doesn't want anything to do with me or my brothers."

Gabriel did not want to elaborate further. They sat in silence for a while. Daniel wondered why his mother and father got divorced. Did he cheat too like Gabriel's father? Did he try to reconcile as well and did his mother refuse? Daniel could only imagine because his mother never spoke of his father or of the divorce.

"I won! I won! I won!!" Rigoberto yelled out as he hurriedly rushed towards the kitchen.

Daniel and Gabriel went to see what the commotion was all about.

Chapter Four

# Clam Hunting

As he sat in his second period honors history class taught by Mrs. Cooper, Daniel quickly noticed that his fellow black students were increasingly getting agitated as the day's discussion continued. Mrs. Cooper had assigned each eighth grade class to watch the rerun of the miniseries Roots that was being aired in commemoration of its upcoming sequel. The sequel would be airing in two more weeks during the middle of February 1979. Every day Mrs. Cooper would ask questions about the week-long assignment and the emotional response thickened the air in the classroom. She posed provocative questions during every history class which she had issued this assignment. The questions that Wednesday morning were about episode two of the miniseries. The particular scene being discussed involved Kunta Kinte's refusal to accept his slave name, Toby, because he wanted to preserve his Mandinka warrior heritage. After several unsuccessful attempts to escape, the white plantation overseer gathered all of the slaves and ordered one of the slaves to whip Kunta repeatedly until he relented from the beatings and finally acknowledged his new slave name. Some of the black students were seriously, visibly upset when other students during the discussion described the scene in great detail. They had to relive the brutal memory from the prior night's viewing.

"Can someone tell me if they were in Kunta's place, what would they do?" Mrs. Cooper inquired.

"I would kick his ass," one of the other students nervously blared out, but with hardened resolve.

"No you wouldn't. You're too chicken to do anything now! What makes you think you would grow a pair once you were a slave?" another student interjected.

The rest of the students gasped or laughed at this last remark, having known the first student's character over the years. Some knew him since elementary school. Mrs. Cooper quickly hushed the class and walked around the room observing her students.

"Only serious responses. I want a respectful discussion today; otherwise I will assign detention to those who will not mind my words. And do raise your hand first. I will not tolerate any disruptive behavior." Mrs. Cooper sternly asserted her control over the classroom, but at the same time she tried to reassure her students that it was okay for them to openly discuss their thoughts and feelings.

The discussion continued and Daniel remained uncharacteristically silent during most of it. He did not want to add anything that could be misconstrued or misunderstood by his fellow students. Instead, he listened quietly, seated in the front of the class as usual. He had watched all of the episodes aired so far and was appalled by the treatment of the Mandika people who were unwillingly brought as slaves to the States from Gambia. In all honesty, Daniel could not wrap his head around the concept of slavery and the slave trade and why people would willing engage in such behavior and subject others to such brutality. He did not believe that he had anything substantive to contribute at the time. He was glad when the class period was finally over because the day's discussion was emotionally draining and overwhelming. He tried to forget it as he continued going about his day. He avoided getting involved in any spontaneous discussions occurring in the exterior hallways when the students at

Hosler Junior High School switched classes after each period. Daniel also avoided the topic during his lunch period and quietly sat by himself. He chose not to sit near Gabriel or his other friends; not even Jonathan Clarke. They were not in Daniel's history class with Mrs. Cooper so they were unaware of what was bothering Daniel. His friends had also not watched the series themselves. Daniel's friends left him alone during the lunch period as well as the remaining two periods of the school day.

Daniel was finally relieved when his last period ended and he could go home. However, he had to stop at his locker in front of Mr. Lucas's classroom and leave some of his belongings inside his locker that he did not need that evening. After doing so, Daniel proceeded across the grassy area and then past the track field near the southeastern corner of the school. He exited the eastern gate leading to Bullis Road and then walked to the long block north past the library towards Century Boulevard. He turned right onto Century Boulevard and continued walking east past Earnestine Avenue and then past Hulme Avenue. He walked lazily as Century Boulevard turned south until he reached Muriel Drive. He crossed the busy boulevard alone and walked along Muriel Drive until it became Beechwood Avenue. As he reached the corner of Beechwood Avenue and Shirley Avenue, he saw several black males in the distance from his school. They were punching and kicking one of his white classmates. Daniel could barely recognize him as Alex Anderson.

"This is for Kunta!!" one of the black classmates said as he tried to kick Alex in the stomach.

"This is for my ancestors who your family enslaved. You aren't going to enslave me, you bastard," said another. This student also kicked Alex repeatedly, sometimes aiming at his stomach or his legs or back. The other boys laughed and mocked as they continued their callous assault.

"What are you doing? Stop hitting him," Daniel yelled from across the street. He ran up to the boys and stopped them from kicking Alex. Daniel pulled them off of Alex one by one. The other boys then ran off, each in their own direction. Daniel reached down to give Alex a hand so that he could get up from the sidewalk. Alex was laying on the ground in a fetal position, protecting his stomach and other sensitive areas. Once on his feet, Alex slowly and painfully dusted his jeans off. His frail, skinny body seemed alright for the most part. "Are you alright? Did they hurt you? I'm sorry about what they did. They had no right to hurt you. You had nothing to do with it."

After a brief pause, he said, "I'm Alex." Alex offered his hand and the two shook. Daniel already knew his name from around school, but the two never spoke before. They were never introduced to each other and had no mutual friends.

"I'm Daniel. Are you sure that you are alright?"

"I'm a little sore. I'm just glad that you stopped them." Alex looked around the sidewalk, found his glasses, bent over to pick them up, and put them on. "My house is just right there." He pointed to the second house on Shirley Avenue, just east of where the two boys were standing. "I'll be alright. Thanks again."

Daniel watched as Alex walked to his house. He kept on watching until Alex had opened the door and safely entered undisturbed. Daniel waited a few minutes to see if the other boys returned. When they did not, he then proceeded on Beechwood Avenue until it banked right towards Atlantic Avenue. Daniel kept walking another fifteen to twenty minutes until he arrived at his own house on Chambers Lane near the corner of Louise Avenue. He slept with some difficulty that night, bothered by the day's events. He refused to watch that night's episode of Roots. It was too much for him to endure. He planned to continue watching the show again the next night so that he could get a good grade on the assignment. Daniel knew that Mrs. Cooper liked him because he was the top student in her class. He knew that she would excuse his missing that night's episode. At least he had hoped so. He was right when he told Mrs. Cooper about it the next day.

In the ensuing weeks, Daniel would see Alex sitting alone in the cafeteria. The first few times, Daniel walked past him and would sit with Gabriel and Jonathan. Daniel would eat lunch with them. He would oftentimes sneak a glance toward Alex and wonder what he was thinking or what his family thought when he arrived home that afternoon a little bruised. Daniel did not know Alex very well. Daniel wondered if Alex would have told the truth about the assault and the reasons why or whether Alex would have made an excuse, such as he clumsily fell which was typical of his teenage awkwardness. Daniel tried to ignore such silly thoughts and tried to engage conversation with Jonathan and Gabriel. Jonathan waxed on as he always did about his concerns about communism and its potential world domination and how America should do whatever it could to stop the spread of communism. Daniel did not feel like listening to Jonathan's incessant politicking. He sat there pretending to listen and nodding on occasion so that Jonathan's feelings would not get hurt. Jonathan always hated when his friends did not take him seriously. Jonathan wanted to be president someday.

Daniel resolved to speak with Alex so that he could find out how he was doing. So instead of walking at his typical fast pace home after school, Daniel lingered around for a few minutes until he saw Alex exiting the eastern gate on Bullis Road. Daniel slowly and nonchalantly walked behind him a few feet. As they both began to approach Century Boulevard, Daniel said, "Hey, Alex. Wanna go into Thrifty's for some ice cream? My treat."

"Sure. That would be nice."

Daniel walked quickly to catch up to Alex. They crossed the street, entered the store, and each coincidentally ordered a double scoop of pistachio ice cream. Daniel paid with his lunch money. The two boys continued walking home together.

When they reached Shirley Avenue, Alex asked, "One of these days, you should come over for dinner."

"I would like that," Daniel responded. They waved goodbye and went their separate ways.

The following weekend, Daniel walked to Alex's house in the afternoon. Alex was expecting him. When Daniel knocked on the door, Alex's younger sister, Tara, answered. "Who are you?" Tara's small stature meant that Daniel had to look down to see her. Her scraggly blond hair almost covered her face. She brushed it aside with her left hand so that she could see him better. Daniel knelt somewhat and replied, "I'm Alex's friend. Is he here?"

She turned slightly around and yelled, "Alex!!! Someone's at the door for you. I thought you don't have any friends?" She looked back at Daniel and smiled.

"Quit yelling. You know this house is small and everyone can hear you." Alex galloped to the living room and opened the door wider so that Daniel could walk inside. Daniel entered the cozy yet disheveled house. As he did, Alex's younger brother, Thomas, entered the room. Thomas was eight years old and Tara was six.

"I'm Tommy." He reached out his hand to introduce himself. "I didn't know we were having company today."

"You don't have to approve. Dad does," Alex added.

Just then, Alex's dad, an older gray-haired white male around his mid-forties, came out from behind everyone and introduced himself to Daniel. He had the similar accent that Daniel's neighborhood friend, Randy, had. Randy was from Oklahoma and had recently moved back there earlier that school year. Daniel thought that perhaps Alex's father was also from there.

"Don't mind the kids. They're just excited. That's all." Alex's father started gathering a few buckets and an ice cooler. "Alex, help your brother take these and put them in the wagon." Daniel watched and the two boys complied.

Mr. Anderson tried his best to comb Tara's hair, but she resisted and fiddled so that she could get away. Her father was accustomed to her unfruitful efforts. Daniel got the impression that this was how she always responded to her father's grooming attempts. "Stay still," he added and turned to Daniel, "I hope you don't mind, but we're going clam hunting for our dinner tonight."

"It's not just clams. There are also mussels and other shellfish. I can't wait," interjected Tommy. Daniel had not realized that he had hurriedly returned from the station wagon.

"I've never gone clam hunting before." Daniel was excited about this new experience. Alex had not told him about this excursion either. "I didn't bring my swimming trunk."

"No worries. They let you swim in your shorts. That's how we all are going to do it," Alex remarked.

They gathered into the station wagon to head off clam hunting. Alex and Daniel were seated in the rear facing seats at the back of the wagon. Tommy and Tara were in the back seat. Their father was seated in the front seat alone with the buckets and cooler placed on the front passenger seat. As the vehicle was about to drive off, Daniel asked, "Is your mother going to come with us?"

Alex hesitated, but replied, "She doesn't live with us. She moved out a couple of years after Tara was born."

Daniel had not realized this and he tried to switch the topic so that the boys could still have a great Sunday afternoon going clam hunting. The two chatted continuously until Mr. Anderson drove the station wagon into a parking lot, paid the $5 per vehicle fee, and parked his vehicle in the first available spot closest to the lagoon. Daniel had never been to this lagoon before. It was apparently only a short ride from his house, but he never really knew where because he was too busy talking to Alex to notice.

Tommy and Tara bolted out of the station wagon and ran into the lagoon without hesitating. They were splashing the water with their little hands and feet before Mr. Anderson was able to forewarn them to be careful. He knew that his children were aware of the posted rules because he had brought them here innumerable times before. It was a Sunday family tradition of sorts. Alex and Daniel carried the ice cooler to the water's edge and sat it on a sandy area near the car. Mr. Anderson handed them both each a small bucket and placed the remaining three buckets down.

"What's this for?" Daniel inquired.

"We put the clams and mussels in them, silly." Alex was surprised as to how Daniel was known to be smart in school but naive when it came to something so simple as clam hunting.

"So, the clams are in the lagoon?"

"Yes, just use your hand, dig around the sand, and when you find one, pull it up." Alex demonstrated how to do it in the air.

Daniel took off his shirt and entered the tepid waters. Alex entered nearly fully clothed. They each swam and played and occasionally hunted for clams during their time there. There were about ten other people in the lagoon. All had paid for the privilege of going clam hunting, but most were enjoying the fresh and cool waters of the lagoon. After a few hours, the buckets were filled with pismo and purple clams, mussels, one or two razor clams and an occasional piece of kelp, especially in the bucket that little Tara filled.

Daniel could not believe how fast the time passed and how soon he would have to leave this lagoon. He watched intently out the back of the wagon as Mr. Anderson drove away. Shortly thereafter, they arrived at their house on Shirley Avenue and unloaded the wagon. As they were doing so, Mr. Anderson had placed a portable outdoor camping grill on that part of the front lawn where there was not any grass. It was an area of about six feet in diameter where there was nothing but dirt or weeds because the front lawn had been neglected for a long time. Mr. Anderson placed some wood and charcoal under the folding grill and lite it. It slowly began to burn. He went back into the house and brought out a large, twenty-quart pot filled with water and placed it on the grill, letting the open flames boil the water. When the water boiled over, he placed some of the clams and mussels in and pulled them out once they were done. Each of the kids, including Daniel, ate the clams and mussels with drizzled, melted butter on them.

Alex went inside the house and brought out a few dozen radishes. He handed one to Daniel and began eating the one in his hand. "Eat it. You'll like it."

Daniel had never eaten radishes before. He bit into the cool, purple and red root, crunching it as he ate. The combined meal was delicious. Alex and his family stood around the front yard in their makeshift claim boil, laughing and joking and eating and enjoying the lazy early evening. Daniel observed Mr. Anderson playing with Tara and Tommy and thought to himself, "I guess this is what it means to have a father."

Chapter Five

# Thanksgiving

Daniel sat in the principal's office awaiting Mrs. Campbell's entrance. He was summoned to be there after his sixth period math class with Mr. Kumano. He nervously thought of anything that he could be in trouble for. Maybe it was the time he and Gabriel were playing finger football during lunch and Daniel was trying to make a point after touchdown. He flicked the triangle-shaped paper "football", but instead of flying through the goal post made with Gabriel's finger, it sliced to the right and almost hit Regina Simpleton in the eye. She vowed to get them in trouble. But that was six weeks ago. Daniel thought that surely something would have happened to him sooner if that was why he was in trouble. Maybe it was the time that he was playing the handheld Mattel basketball electronic game outside of Mr. Lucas's class. Daniel's fingers rapidly pushed the four red directional arrows and the blue basket buttons so furiously that the continued scoring caused the repeated high-pitched artificial goal sound to emanate into the classroom because the doors were opened. Mr. Lucas rushed out of the room and told Daniel to stop because the whole class could hear him. Or maybe it was during P.E. when his class was practicing the various swimming strokes (freestyle, butterfly, breast-stroke and side-stroke). While swimming in the middle of the pool, Daniel pretended to have a leg cramp, causing everyone to stop swimming. The lifeguard, a cute high schooler named Jennifer Morris, had to jump in the pool and rescue him. Sitting in Mrs. Campbell's office, Daniel giggled at the thought of the pool prank. At the time, he was happy to get the opportunity to look deeply into Jennifer's eyes rather than just admiring her from afar like the other eight grade boys in Mrs. Garcia's P.E. class. Mrs. Garcia was not amused though. Fortunately, his gym teacher did not bother to send Daniel to the principal's office. She ignored the incident as if it never happened. Jennifer just smiled at Daniel. He was in ecstasy and his impression easily betrayed it. The other boys watched with envy and admiration in their eyes. Daniel was the talk of the entire school for a few days until some other newsworthy event at Hosler Junior High took its place. Something newsworthy happened practically every week.

As Daniel's thoughts meandered, just then, Mrs. Campbell briskly walked into her office with a manila folder in her hand. She sat down on a seat adjacent to the one Daniel was sitting on near the door and looked at him directly in the eyes. "Mr. Mendoza. It's the end of the school year and I've been reviewing your grades. The graduation ceremony is coming up shortly and I've been talking to all of the top students for the class of 1979 about what is expected of them during the promotion ceremony."

Daniel sat attentively because he was still a little confused about what was his purpose for being in her office. He wanted her to get to the point quickly, but knew never to interrupt her. No one interrupted Mrs. Campbell; not even the school superintendent.

"Because you are in the top of your class, you will be seated in the front of the platform with the rest of the top ten students. You will need to get to the school about thirty minutes earlier so that you will be in your proper position during the processional. You also get two extra tickets to the ceremony so that you can invite more of your family," Mrs. Campbell continued.

Daniel had no knowledge that there were any special recognition for the top ten students. His brother, Jose Luis, graduated the year before from Hosler, but Daniel did not attend. He also did not attend when his sister, Maria, graduated two years earlier. Daniel asked her, "What's my ranking?"

"Well, you're ranked third."

"Third?!! I want to be number one," Daniel believed that he was thinking this to himself. He had actually said it aloud and Mrs. Campbell heard him.

"I know that you are an excellent student. You are driven and could have been number one except for some B grades that you received. You lack focus at times. I'm not sure that Mr. Zepeda has been a good influence on you. Why are you so driven, Daniel?"

The question made him pensive. He sat quietly, thinking to himself whether he should tell Mrs. Campbell about what truly motivated him to exceed in school. Daniel never trusted adults enough to share his intimate feelings. There was nothing special about Mrs. Campbell that would engender his trust. He did not know her that well. He was not sure if she even liked him that much or respected him. Something deep inside said not to trust her, but despite that innate feeling, Daniel began to speak.

He described the front porch of the yellow, quaint two-bedroom house. Daniel and Jose Luis slept on their separate twin beds in the living room that their mother turned into a makeshift bedroom for them. It was directly off of the kitchen. Maria and Sylvia shared the bedroom in the rear of the house and their mother had the master bedroom in the front. The porch faced directly towards Serrano Avenue and faced a large, ill peach tree whose fruit revealed its sickness every spring. But when Daniel wanted to escape the family drama and the lack of privacy not afforded in his shared bedroom, he would sit on the porch. He hoped no one would come by so that he could think without the normal disturbances. On the particular evening that his mind focused on, Daniel was sitting alone on the porch after a long, filling Thanksgiving dinner. He was solemn and mirthless; more like despondent and depressed. His eyes were still glazed from imbibing the Cold Duck during the early meal. In fact, a bottle of the cheap, South Australian sparkling wine was uncomfortably in his left hand. The bottle was still almost full. Daniel would slowly take a half-swig on occasion even though it was difficult to do so because of his trembling.

As the alcohol warmed his body with each sip, it also stung internally and externally the way warm water hurts when placed on an open wound. Daniel's mind could not distinguish the internal, invisible wounds from those bruises and welts that his back, arms, and legs sustained. He recently sustained these injuries from the swift, multiple swats with a thick, tanned leather belt, which was weather-worn as if harvested from an old bull. He could still feel the echo of it pounding on his flesh. Daniel's mother had never used corporeal punishment before. It was the first time in what would turn out to be many more times when she would physically punish Daniel. What made it more unbearable was that the corporal punishment was not a result of anything that Daniel had done. Instead, when the mischievous and immature Jose Luis had decided to destroy a few of his toys because their mother refused to buy him any new ones, Mrs. Mendoza decided to not only punish him, but to also punish Maria and Daniel. They did not do anything to prevent it. In Mrs. Mendoza's mind the other children were equally guilty for allowing Jose Luis to destroy his toys. Daniel believed it was exceedingly unfair to be punished for something that he had not done. He also had no way of preventing it because he was unaware that his older brother was even destroying any toys. Neither Daniel nor Maria were present when Jose Luis did so. When they saw Jose Luis gleefully smiling after they were beaten for his actions, it only infuriated them even more. That would not be the last time that Maria and Daniel would be unfairly punished for Jose Luis's actions.

Off in the distance, it was as if a subliminal voice was asking Daniel how that horrid experience affected his educational aspirations. It was unclear whether someone had in fact asked Daniel a question or if a still small voice inside of him did. Despite not knowing whether he was just dreaming or truly talking to Mrs. Campbell, Daniel's scrambled thoughts continued in spite of the haze. As he pictured himself still sitting on the porch at the young age of nine years old, he could hear the front door open. Maria also came outside looking for him. He was puzzled by that decision. She sat near him on the porch and asked for a sip of wine. Daniel reluctantly agreed and handed her the bottle, which she took willingly. They sat there without speaking further until the silence was broken by Daniel.

"Mom really hasn't been herself lately." He did not want to mention the day's beating aloud although Maria was already aware of it given that she suffered through it too. He thought to do so explicitly would somehow validate it or acknowledge that it occurred. Daniel preferred to be in self-denial even though the pain was real. Perhaps the dulling of the wine made it seem less real, but the throbbing of his little body betrayed that denial. "I don't know why she's being this way," he continued.

"I do."

"Well, tell me."

"It's obvious. Mom's unhappy."

Daniel quickly glanced over to her and listened more attentively. "Why is she so unhappy?"

Daniel knew that he had recently told his mother that he had seen her boyfriend, Marcelo, with another woman. Daniel may have forgotten that at the time. He did not really know that such adult issues last more than a day. They were unlike problems that pre-teen boys typically have which seem to magically disappear every morning and something new takes its place. Every issue on Daniel's mind was fleeting and non-existence except for the new found issue that he was struggling with now and which would not disappear even after the wounds healed. But Marcelo's cheating was not what Maria mentioned as the source of their mother's unhappiness. What she said was something totally unknown to him.

"Mom told me why she is unhappy. She's unhappy because she wouldn't have to deal with these relationship issues if she was still married to our dad." Daniel was perplexed at Maria's explanation. "And do you know why our dad left? He left because he only wanted two kids and then you came along. He didn't want three kids. When mom became pregnant with you, dad didn't want to deal with it any more. Two kids were enough so he left. Mom blames you for our dad leaving. She resents you. And now this thing with Sylvia's father, she resents you even more."

Maria decided to stop talking. She could sense Daniel's increased despondency so she stood up and walked back inside without saying another word or letting Daniel ask her any questions. She had no further answers. Daniel did not feel like letting her know what he was thinking or feeling anyway. It would only make things worse. Daniel's thoughts continued to race. He pictured his father leaving, but he had no knowledge of what his father looked like. Daniel had never seen a picture of his father before. Daniel knew that his mind was playing tricks on him, that he could not trust any of these purported memories that were dangling about in his head. The only thing that was real to him was the emptiness that filled his body like the hollowing out of a tree that ultimately collapses from its own weight. Despite his mental gymnastics to reassure himself that things would be okay, that he was okay, nothing brightened his spirit. He struggled to lay ahold of something, anything, that would tether his soul to a glimmer of reality, but his youthful mind was too inexperienced to succeed, too weakened by intoxication. The only thing that could help and dull the pain even further was more of it. So he held the nearly full bottle of sparkling wine tightly to his lips, swallowing the remaining wine all at once. This, however, did not make things better. He went inside, stumbled to his bed and fell asleep.

In that moment, it was as if the overarching haze that dimmed his mind was finally lifted and he could see clearly again. His eyes focused ahead of him again. Mrs. Campbell stared at him puzzled by his demeanor.

"Go on. Might as well continue," she added as she patiently waited for Daniel to speak again.

"I didn't feel loved by my mother at that moment. I knew she couldn't love me if I was the source of her unhappiness. I wanted her to love me and the only thing that I could think of that may make her love me was to make something of myself."

"What do you mean?"

"Well, if I did well in school, became someone that she respected, that would make her feel proud of me and then she would want to love me." Daniel sighed after finally admitting this for the first time aloud to anyone and to himself. He hoped Mrs. Campbell would be more understanding and less critical of his thinking.

After Daniel made that promise to himself that Thanksgiving, his educational experience changed. He worked hard and studied harder. He went from being an above average student to a straight A student; excelling in everything that he did. The self-imposed drive that Mrs. Campbell mentioned was tremendously stressful for a young boy. But Daniel's academic success never seemed to make his mother feel closer to him or love him as he mistakenly thought. He was not deterred. Although in the back of his mind, Daniel knew that it would never make a difference. A part of him hoped that perhaps one day when he finally met his father, maybe his father would appreciate Daniel's hard work and success. But that was not only a long shot, but also something that even Daniel could not convince himself to believe. Despite that, Daniel needed something to hope for because he felt alone and estranged in his family.

That Thanksgiving was the last time Daniel drank any alcohol.

# Chapter Six

# Lamont

As the slightly dilapidated Greyhound bus began its slow and bumpy ride along Interstate 5, the low hum of its air conditioning units not only filled the interior of the bus with cool, refreshing air, but also gave a sense of comfort to those weary and experienced passengers. Most of the passengers were keenly aware that the eight hour drive north towards Bakersfield would be blanketed by the harsh, summer sun throughout the duration of the trip. They gladly welcomed its relief. Inexperienced travelers like the Mendoza family were unexpectedly cold and cautiously leery of the nearly full bus. The brown pleather seats were tattered in places, but were still supple enough to allow for a respectable and comfortable ride. This Greyhound bus was unlike the various RTD buses ridden by the Mendoza family for their local travels to the dentist or to the children's hospital when Maria's asthma acted up or other routine trips that they had to take. RTD buses typically smelled of urine from the many homeless riders that would take the bus during the early mornings and mysteriously disappear to whatever locations suited them that day. The Mendoza children loathed traveling on RTD buses. Their mother had no car and that was the only mode of transportation available. They knew upon entering the Greyhound bus that they would certainly enjoy this trip.

The trip was not without its concerns. Noise from the occasional laughter of small children broke any silence, disturbing anyone's hasty attempt to sleep on the bus, including Mrs. Mendoza who preferred to sleep after an anxious night in anticipation of their trip. An arguing young Mexican couple in the rear of the bus near the internal toilet were told by two or three passengers to calm down and stop fighting; eventually the bus driver had to get involved. People often switched seats to avoid the beating sun, but by doing so they would frequently bump into another passenger's elbow or back; making those on the aisle seat guarded and alert. Every so often, passengers would burst out in song to pass the time away. But the young man in the left middle of the bus was stuck on the same lyrics and repeated them over and over again like a broken record. His whiny voice would blare out "Shadow dancing, baby you do it right…Shadow dancing" as if he was on key and a real member of the band. The song was popular in the summer of 1978 and everyone on the bus was tired of hearing it by then.

But what made the long trip more bearable despite any myriad distractions were the host of treats that Mrs. Mendoza packed in a large brown, paper grocery bag. The treats were supposed to alleviate any hunger pains that her three children had. She expected that the Greyhound bus would not stop for any length of time during its voyage to allow those riders to disembark and eat a proper lunch. Mrs. Mendoza expected that the bus would only briefly stop every hour or so at each bus station to drop off or take on more passengers. This would only allow those existing passengers little or no time to enjoy the stop. One of Mrs. Mendoza's coworkers forewarned her of this short coming. In anticipation, she packed several ding dongs, zingers, moon pies, Dolly Madison fruit pies, and, of course, Sylvia's favorite snack, animal crackers. Mrs. Mendoza anticipated that her oldest son, Jose Luis, would constantly pester her for snacks, but she did not have the time to pre-make any bologna sandwiches before this last minute trip was planned. Instead, she spent most of the previous night ensuring that her children packed properly. Her other children would not mind the lack of anything substantial to eat. They would be anxiously awaiting their arrival to the final destination and would leave her alone. The Mendoza family had never been north of Los Angeles before. For the past few years, the family primarily stayed near and around the family home on Chambers Lane. This trip was a rare family treat and they were all excited.

Sylvia, however, was not disappointed that she was not going to Lamont for the weekend. She was happy to spend the weekend alone with her father as most six year olds would be. Mrs. Mendoza was reluctant to bring her to see Regino Mendoza, the patriarch of the Mendoza family and the father of Jose Luis Mendoza, Senior. Sylvia was born seven years after Lucia Mendoza divorced her first husband, Jose Luis, and Sylvia was not related. Although Mrs. Mendoza had not seen Regino in the intervening years, she knew that he was a conservative Puerto Rican man who would not want to be reminded of the failed marriage so explicitly. He had not seen his grandchildren since the divorce and that was the only focus on his mind. Sylvia's absence gave the other children the rare opportunity to get attention from their mother which was typically reserved for the youngest child, her favorite. It was only a matter of time over the long week that their mother would warm up to them or at least they hoped. Now, she was tired, hungry, sleepy, and relegated herself to stingily handing out the occasional snack.

So the children busied themselves in their own separate way. Maria found another fifteen year old girl, Annalise, to talk to. She moved to the front of the bus and sat next to her. But that was not until the first stop when Annalise's family got on in Maywood. The two sat next to each other the entire trip. Annalise's family was headed to Visalia where her uncle and his family worked. Jose Luis, Junior played with his Six Million Dollar Man action figure. He would look at passengers through its bionic eye as if he had x-ray vision. Jose Luis would also push the trigger on the back of the action figure and make its arm lift snacks so that he could eat them. He would also roll back the skin on the right arm and change the bionic elements. He quickly bored of the toy and eventually threw it aside almost hitting a boy. Jose Luis denied doing it on purpose and refused to apologize even after his mother vehemently asked him too. He regretted that decision because, at the next stop, Mrs. Mendoza punished him and the other children as a result. His left ear was still red and sore where she vigorously tugged at it to get his attention.

Daniel would solemnly look out the window dreaming of the many places that whisked by. Most were indistinguishable. The first noticeable thing that caught his eye was the recently-opened, white wooden roller coaster that loomed large on the horizon as the Greyhound bus headed north towards the hills of Valencia. The roller coaster trains would speedily rumble and sway along the dual tracks. Daniel was amazed at its size, but would be unaware of the tragedy occurring later that year when a young woman was thrown from the roller coaster.

The bus continued its slow, meandering climb up Interstate 5 and began approaching Lake Castaic. As it did so, Daniel arose from his seat like any of the other passengers and gathered towards the windows on the right side of the bus so that he could get a better view of the lake. He could see a swimming beach at the lower lagoon of the lake. He could see individuals fishing in both the upper and lower parts of the lake. One fisherman was in a float tube fishing in the lower lake.

"I wonder what they are catching," Daniel inquired.

"They are bass fishing," said an older gentleman. As Daniel looked over towards the voice, he could see the man gently pushing his straw hat downward to cover his eyes.

"How do you know? I couldn't see any fish."

"Because I used to go bass fishing at Castaic Lake with my family since I was about your age, I think." Daniel thought the man must have led a privileged life if he could be out in this beautiful area, which Daniel had never seen before. He wondered why the man was now traveling by Greyhound.

Soon, Daniel moved on to other things and other distractions. By the time the bus reached Grapevine by the Tejon Pass, he had fallen asleep. Jose Luis continued irritating the other passengers on board and Maria was still talking with Annalise about nothing really important. In no time, the Greyhound bus stopped at its final destination at a bus station in the southwestern part of Bakersfield. The bus driver informed everyone that they had to disembark and gather their things. He opened the bottom compartments where the luggage was stored so that the passengers could get their luggage. Everyone did. When the compartments were all empty, Jose Luis realized that he had forgotten to bring his suitcase and that he had left it at home. He pretended that he had grabbed it from the bus, hoping that his mother would not find out. However, he knew that it would only be a matter of time before she would find out because they were staying at his grandfather's house for nearly a week. He would have to do something about the lack of clothing. Jose Luis did not worry about it and would deal with it when it came. He thought probably Wednesday at the latest.

A station wagon pulled up to the Greyhound bus station and when the doors opened, Regino Mendoza exited the vehicle. His dark brown, wavy hair complemented his even darker, black skin. From afar, Regino looked like an African American male. His wavy hair was naturally so and made his appearance distinctive. Once he spoke Spanish with a fast, Puerto Rican dialect, it was unmistakable that Regino was unusual. His appearance was in contrast to the Mendoza children because the children were a lighter shade of brown, typical of Hispanic children.

As the children were unloading their things from the bus, Julia Mendoza, Regino's wife and their grandmother, exited the station wagon. The mystery of the differing coloration was solved. Julia was a light pale, Puerto Rican woman more akin to women from Spain, perhaps even Madrid or Barcelona. Her milky white skin was lighter than anyone in the family. It was obvious that their father, Jose Luis, Senior, and his offspring, who were now packing into the station wagon, were an amalgamation of the different hues that their grandparents had. The Puerto Rican people were a combination of Spanish Europeans, Taino Indians, and African slaves brought to the island. This cultural intertwining was even more obvious when the station wagon arrived ten minutes later at Regino's house and Regino's younger children greeted the Mendoza kids from Chambers Lane. They too had a mixture of hues. The oldest daughter, who was also named Julia, had her mother's pale white skin and long, flowing black hair. The only boy, Regino, Junior, had the same complexion as the Mendoza children. Margarita Mendoza, the youngest daughter was somewhat darker than Regino, Junior and the other siblings, but not by much. None of Regino's younger, second set of children had his dark-hued skin. He was very proud of that.

After they all greeted each other in the quaint living room, they entered the large backyard. Roaming near the back chain-linked fence was a ninety pound suckling pig. It would occasionally eat the grass and snort loudly as if he knew that his fateful day was today. At first the Mendoza children were unaware of the pig until their grandfather said in Spanish that he was planning on killing the pig so that he could have a traditional Puerto Rican pig roast in celebration of their arrival. Their younger uncle and aunts had to translate for them in order for them to understand. Maria was shocked and appalled that a live pig would be slaughtered. She entered the house to avoid it. Mrs. Mendoza followed shortly thereafter. Daniel, however, was enthralled with the idea and followed his grandfather closely. Mr. Mendoza poked a knife in the young pig's neck while Margarita held a worn, white pot to collect its blood. Regino, Junior and Julia were holding the pig down tightly. In moments, the life blood was totally drained and the pig was lifeless.

The children then scurried to assist their father in de-hairing the pig. Margarita took the pot of blood to her mother in the kitchen and exchanged it for another pot containing scalding water. She brought the second pot quickly to her father. Regino lapped the hot water onto the pig with a ladle and then scraped the hair off with a sharp knife. After most of the back was de-haired, he let his son do the rest. Mr. Mendoza went inside to help his wife, Julia, prepare for dinner. By the time everyone realized what was going on, the pig was splayed on a long wooden stick used as a makeshift rotisserie. Before lighting the wood logs, Julia lathered the pig with adobo mojado made of crushed garlic, black pepper, salt, orégano brujo, olive oil, and a little red wine vinegar. She stuffed some of the adobo into the numerous slits that were cut along various parts of the body so that the flavor would meld deeper into the meat making it even more succulent. The aroma from the adobo filled the backyard until the intense fragrance from the crackling mesquite wood intermingled with it, making more of a pervasive and familiar scent reminiscent of similar roastings on the island, especially around Christmas time. Every fifteen minutes or so, Regino, Junior would turn the pig and also baste it with additional adobo while doing so. This was his job for the next six hours or so. He often enjoyed it but wanted this time to spend with his new-found nephews and niece.

In the meantime, everyone else was in the kitchen. All of the Mendoza children were watching and enjoying the cooking festivities that their grandparents and aunts were doing. It was like a choreographed production rehearsed many times over the years. A pot of white rice was on the stove. The rice was stirred into the pot of pig's blood that had already been mixed with salt, cilantro, chili peppers, and garlic. Margarita and Julia took turns inserting a funnel into fresh pig intestines, stuffing them with the blood and rice mixture. The stuffed intestines were boiled in salted water for about a half an hour.

"What are you making?" Daniel asked excitedly.

His mother answered, "They are making morcilla."

"What's that?" asked Jose Luis.

"It's Puerto Rican blood sausage."

"Sound delicious," Daniel added.

"Yuck," Maria exclaimed. Her disgust was obvious.

Jose Luis was silent. He would ultimately try it, but he pretended to be aloof, which was unnatural for his usual greedy predilection.

When the boiling was done, Julia drained the water, cut some of the morcilla into small pieces, and fried them in coconut oil until they were a golden brown. The rest of the morcilla, she put into the freezer for later use. Julia let the morcilla cool down on top of paper towels and then cupped one in her hand, walked over to Daniel, and let him bite into it. It was delicious. She served the rest of it with tostones and it was quickly consumed.

By the end of the night, everyone's belly was full with chicharrones, pork shoulder, jowl, crispy pig ears, and other sundry, tasty pieces of pig. Regino, Senior had eaten the tail all by himself. Julia had set aside the entire head (except the ears) to make a Puerto Rican-styled head cheese. The refrigerator was filled with various pieces of the pig and would be eaten for most of the meals that week that the Mendoza family stayed in Lamont.

Chapter Seven

# Uncle Louie

The Bermuda grass was still soppy from the morning dew, but it was wildly overgrown enough that it was heavily uneven throughout the yard. The grass began to grow into the cracks of the slightly crumbling front walkway, making the yard look more like a teenage boy's unkept hair that had not been combed or trimmed in months. As the wheels of the push mower slowly turned and moved backwards and forwards, the wet grass would fling to the sides. This had the benefit of giving Daniel the ability to rake the cut grass into large clumps that could be easily placed into green hefty bags. The bags would be later thrown on the sidewalk for the garbage collectors to pick up the following morning. Jose Luis continued pushing the mower with little determination. His only motivation was the knowledge that if he did not finish the yard work by the early afternoon, his mother would bring out a switch. Lucia made the switch from the granny apple tree in the very front of the yard. She would spank him haphazardly if Jose Luis would not complete his chores. The knots on the thin, long branch though small could still cause bruises and welts that lasted for nearly a week. Even at fourteen years old, Jose Luis was still afraid of his mother. She was over a foot shorter than he was and more frail given her diminutive stature. So Jose Luis persisted in this mundane chore while dreaming of other adventures that he could be doing at that moment.

Such Sunday mornings were no longer filled with attending mass at St. Luke's Catholic Church. Lucia Maria Mendoza had sworn off the Catholic Church years earlier, shortly after she learned of Marcelo's infidelity. By the late summer of 1978, she also stopped forcing her children to attend mass by themselves. She had required her children to go to mass every Sunday these past few years so that she could have some time alone. Instead, Lucia stayed home on Sundays mostly doing nothing. Except for days like today when she was in the rare mood to ensure that her children did each and every household chore that she assigned to them. Her past ambivalence allowed Jose Luis to get away with not mowing the lawn since they returned from Lamont. But that had now come to an end. For some unknown reason, she had become obsessed with the yard. Lucia made her two sons labor that day. She wanted to avoid the neighbors whispering to themselves about the yard's uncleanliness even though the Mendoza house on Chambers Lane was not a part of a homeowners association. Any complaints could never be enforced.

Daniel and Jose Luis had a long day ahead of them and they knew it. They busied themselves trying desperately to finish sooner so they could enjoy the rest of the day. But the amount of work was daunting. They probably could not finish all of it in time anyway. Luckily for them, a red and white 1968 Plymouth Barracuda screeched as it made a sudden U-turn on Chambers Lane to park in front of their house. Both boys looked up as they heard the loud noise and the car grumbled one last time before the owner turned it off and exited the vehicle. The gentleman stood six feet tall with long, dark brown hair that was placed in a single ponytail that hung down past his buttocks. He had very dark skin. His skinny blue jeans were dapper and studded with an occasional rhinestone that glittered as he strolled effortlessly towards the iron gate. He opened the iron gate to enter the chain-linked fence that surrounded the Mendoza family home. He opened the gate with familiarity as if he had been there many times before even though Jose Luis and Daniel had never seen him and did not know who he was. They were silent and perplexed until the gentleman spoke.

"You must be Jose Luis," he said as he walked closer to him, removing his sunglasses and looking up and down at the boy. "And you are Daniel." He smiled and turned his head towards the younger boy.

"Who are you?" Daniel inquired.

Jose Luis remained quiet, eager to hear the stranger's response.

"I'm your father's brother. My name is Louie."

He reached out as if he was going to hug the boys. They were uncertain of whether he was telling the truth because they had never met their father and were reluctant to hug a stranger. Lucia had previously warned them of such dangers. As Jose Luis was about to step back to avoid the hug, the front door opened and he looked towards it.

"Louie, is that you?" Lucia briskly walked towards him. Maria and Sylvia continued following after her when they also exited the front door.

"Hi Lucia. Sorry that I didn't call. Regino gave me your address so I thought I'd stop by while I was in town."

"No worries. You're handsome." She smiled at him the way she would every man, which was often seen as flirting by others, especially by Marcelo.

She had not seen Louie Mendoza since he was about Jose Luis's age. She meet Louie a few times during her short courtship to his brother. Louie had moved to Denver, Colorado for a job once he turned eighteen. So she never saw him again. He was apparently still living in Denver, but was temporarily visiting the Los Angeles area while on his way home from vacationing in Lamont. Louis would visit Lamont once or twice a year so that he could see his parents and younger siblings.

Lucia invited Louie inside and the rest of her children followed them. They sat at the dining room table. Maria brought everyone a glass of iced cold water and sat down on the seat adjacent to her Uncle Louie. She had briefly heard his name while talking with Julia and Margarita about their older siblings while in Lamont earlier that summer. However, her Aunts had no pictures of Louie or any of their older brothers and sisters. So Maria had no idea what her Uncle Louie looked like or what to expect. She was amazed that her uncle looked more like her grandfather, Regino, and had his darker skin, unlike the younger siblings. What amazed Maria even more was Louie's long pony tail. It was reminiscent of the one that she used to have before she cut her hair several years ago to look more mature as a teenager.

The children were excited to meet another family member and had many questions. Why did their uncle move to Denver? Did he like it there? How was the snow? Did he have a wife or kids? What did he do for a living? Did he ever live in New York? Did he have any pictures of their father? Were they close? When did he last see him? Did he know their father's phone number? Will he let them come visit him in Colorado? On and on they asked. Their uncle obliged and answered each question the best that he could until Lucia intervened and stopped them from asking any more questions.

"Okay. That's enough. Your Uncle Louie wants to enjoy his stay here and not be interrogated the whole time."

"That's okay, Lucia. I don't mind."

But the kids knew that once their mother made up her mind that they would have to abide by it or suffer the consequences. So they quickly stopped asking questions.

"How long will you stay?" Lucia asked.

"I'm driving to Denver in the morning."

"You're welcome to spend the night here."

"Thanks. I'll take you up on that." He rose from the dining table and sat on the sofa.

The kids eagerly followed him and quietly fought each other to sit next to him, knowing that their mother was watching the whole ordeal. Sylvia had gone to her room earlier in the conversation because she was feeling somewhat estranged.

"There's enough of me to go around," Louie laughed and gave each child a bear hug starting with Maria. She insisted on having the first hug because she was the oldest child.

Many hours passed and the energy-filled kids never got enough of their long, lost uncle. Because of their abounding interest, Uncle Louie decided that he wanted to do something special for his niece and nephews. After all, he did not know when he would be back in the Los Angeles area again.

"You guys want to go to the movies?" he asked.

"Yes," Maria eagerly responded. The other kids also agreed. Maria rushed into the master bedroom and hastily asked as if she was out of breath, "Can we go? Can we go?"

"Go where?" Lucia puzzlingly inquired.

"Uncle Louie wants to take us to the movies. Can we go?"

He entered the master bedroom along with Jose Luis and Daniel.

"I don't know. It's so late. It's already eleven o'clock." Lucia was reluctant to agree to the last minute request. "How about if instead I promise to take you guys to Colorado to see your Uncle Louie."

The kids were not impressed by their mother's promise. They were well aware that there was very little chance that their mother would keep this promise. She failed to keep almost every promise that she made. Daniel wanted to argue that they had not seen Uncle Louie before, that family is important, and they may never get to see him again, but he knew that his mother would reject his logic as always.

"Come on mom. We never go anywhere. Please," Maria added.

"I promise that I will keep them safe, Lucia," Louie wanted to reassure her and also please the kids. He had just met them, but he felt a kinship to them that went beyond merely their blood connection. Louie had no kids of his own and was not used to the attention. A part of him relished it. He thought that spending more time with them would prolong their attention and affection.

"Well, okay. It's only because Uncle Louie is here. I'll let you guys stay up late and even skip school tomorrow." Lucia was also looking forward to being alone.

"Thanks Mom," Maria said with exuberance. She knew that it was not appropriate to hug her mother or show any outward affection. So she left it at that. The boys also verbally thanked their mother. Sylvia was asleep by then, but she probably would not have been allowed to go given her young age.

"Where is the closest movie theater?" Louie asked.

"There is a Super Saver budget movie theater in Norwalk. It's not too far from here. I'll give you the address," Lucia answered.

Lucia pulled out a yellow pages, looked for the theater ad, and showed Louie the address. He wrote it down and told the kids to meet him inside his Barracuda. They willingly complied and walked single-file towards the front gate. Jose Luis had to quickly return to the house because he forgot his jacket. Although it was late summer, the evenings would get nippy and Jose Luis preferred to double up. He wore two of everything: red gym shorts over his gray sweat pants, a white t-shirt and also a faded yellow-orange shirt over that, and then a gray hoodie. It was a wonder why Jose Luis would sweat more than normal. He had so much clothes on so that he could hide his eczema; the reddish and white rash on his arms and legs was embarrassing according to him. He wrongly believed that the wet sweat may have given his skin the moisture it needed to combat the eczema. So when Louie saw Jose Luis return to the house to put on a blue windbreaker jacket, he was perplexed. Louie, however, thought it better not to mention his newly-found nephew's quirkiness. When all of the kids were piled in the car, Louie wished Lucia a goodnight and then drove the kids to the theater.

The Barracuda roared up Chambers Lane and traveled swiftly to the discount movie theater. The theater as known for playing older movies and some classics. The box office was nearly empty when they arrived because of the lateness of the evening. Only a few movie screens were still showing any movies. Louie purchased tickets to "One Flew Over the Cuckoo's Nest." The kids had never heard of the movie, but were nonetheless happy to be out and about on a Sunday night and with their uncle. No one complained, not even Maria. Uncle Louie also purchased popcorn, soda and various candies, including Goobers and Raisinettes, so that the kids would be able to stay up until almost two o'clock in the morning to see the entire movie.

While his siblings were distracted with their uncle, Daniel watched the movie perplexingly. The host of characters were amusing and unsettling. There was Randle "Mac" McMurphy, the Irish brawler who flouted the strange institution's strict, regimental rules that were enforced by the scary and tyrannical Nurse Ratched. Nurse Ratched was the antithesis of the stereotypical kind, loving nurse that Daniel had always seen on television. There also was the selectively mute, Chief Bromden who was in stark contrast to the sophomoric and impetuous Charlie Cheswick or the oft stuttering Billy Bibbit. For the most part, Daniel did not understand the movie. He struggled to concentrate and stay awake until the final scenes caught his attention.

Once Chief Bromden began to watch Mac being escorted back to his bed and noticed Mac's lack of expression, Daniel perked up and paid closer attention. Daniel noticed that his siblings were already asleep, but he chose not to wake them at this point. He did not want to be distracted and miss the scene. Daniel was startled when he saw scars on Mac's forehead. He knew that something was wrong and that it had to do with Mac's brain and his unresponsiveness. Daniel was too young and inexperienced to know what a lobotomy was. He was aghast when watching the Chief smother Mac with a pillow. Daniel became frightened when he saw Mac's lifeless body lying there. "Why would the Chief do that?" Daniel thought to himself. The once vivacious and pompous Mac had been beaten by the authoritarian regime which he had struggled against. Perhaps the Chief knew that Mac would be unhappy living in such an unfulfilling state. Who could be happy? Certainly, not Daniel.

When the Chief struggled mightily to lift the massive, hydrotherapy console, Daniel was worried that the Chief would not be able to accomplish Mac's escape plan and would end up in the same catatonic state. But when the Chief actually lifted it and hurled the console through a grated window, a sense of euphoria filled Daniel's body. The Chief climbed through the window and determinedly ran off into the horizon, never to be seen again. When another patient woke up and began cheering, Daniel wanted to do the same. Daniel knew that it would be inappropriate. He did not want to be ridiculed by other movie goers or suffer the ire of his siblings should he wake them. So he celebrated the Chief's victory internally as if it was his own. He too knew that he could similarly escape the oppressive confines of Chambers Lane and redetermined to do so. Daniel anxiously awaited as the ending credits scrolled by because he was eager for the next day.

Chapter Eight

# Perry

The loud humming and whirling of the belt sander filled the entire garage and grew even louder especially when the small, six-inch aluminum pipe was pushed sternly against the sanding belt and then side to side while it rested against the level work-table. A bright white and orange line of sparks from the aluminum pipe followed the circumference of the vertical band. Other sparks jetted down and out from the bottom of the worktable like small shooting stars heading in every direction towards the cement garage floor. Any striations in the metal were quickly grinded flat and smooth by the sander, making the polished metal brighter and hotter to the touch. To ensure its smoothness, Perry rubbed his gloved finger over the slightly flattened portion of the pipe. It was not as smooth as he required. So he grinded the pipe some more before switching off the sander and removing his googles to inspect it closer. Because it now met his specifications, Perry clutched the small, lightweight pipe in his hand with some difficulty. Two of his fingers on his right hand, the ring finger and pinky, were missing. He had lost them on separate occasions while doing metalwork at his employer's workshop.

Perry walked a few feet to the floor-standing drill press. He checked to see if the drill bit was securely fastened by grabbing the chuck key that was attached to the drill press with a long, leather holder. Then, starting at the hole in the chuck jaw nearest to him, he inserted the chuck key and tightened it a little. He went around to the next hole and tightened that one. He tightened each consecutive hole a little each time until the chuck jaws were tight on the drill bit like a vice. He then placed the pipe on a wooden v-block that was clamped to the slotted table. Perry pushed the large, front mounted power button to turn the drill press on and lowered the drill bit by slowing turning the feed handle downward until the drill bit pierced both the top and bottom layers of the pipe. He moved the pipe precisely an inch to the left and drilled another hole. When finished, Perry blew on each hole and looked through them. He then grinded some burrs off both holes with the belt sander.

As he was doing this, Daniel slowly approached the garage. He could see Perry standing over the belt sander without wearing any safety ear muffs. Perry was accustomed to the noise by now. His older age, sixty-three, also meant that any hearing loss muffled the sound. It also meant that he did not hear Daniel walking up the long driveway and into the equipment-filled garage. Daniel was aware that Perry would be so engrossed in his work that he did not notice Daniel until Daniel was close enough to be able to touch the equipment. Daniel never dared touching Perry's equipment for fear of upsetting him. Having seen the similar-sized aluminum pipe before with the identically-spaced two holes, Daniel knew that Perry was making another exoskeleton-like device. The device would be manufactured for the various disabled customers that his employer supplied. Although Perry would not be paid for the work that he performed in his garage, this was where Perry would come up with all of the prototypes that his employer manufactured in mass and then sold for a significant price. His employer owned all of the inventions that Perry came up with even though they were exclusively made at his own workshop. Perry's fundamental knowledge of how to manufacture such cutting-edge devices was gained from the intellectual property that he had obtained at work over the past forty plus years. Daniel knew that Perry's employer would own this latest design as well.

Perry did not mind. He simply enjoyed fiddling in his workshop. Any extra royalty income that Perry would have earned from his inventions could have assisted his family in paying for a new car, traveling on vacation, or purchasing a new home now that the demographics of Chambers Lane was slowly changing. Perry sometimes said that he dreamt of buying a home in Arkansas. But that was a lie. Arkansas is where he and his wife, Lois, were originally from. They left Arkansas after Perry graduated technical college after two years and received certifications in welding and metal fabrication. The technical college promised that all of its graduates would be placed in jobs within six months. Perry had no idea that graduating in the top of his class of twenty-three men meant that he could get a lucrative job offer out-of-state at a medical manufacturing company. He received the job offer before he even graduated. Unfortunately, Perry did not bother to do any research about the facility in Downey. He did not even know where Downey was located. He had never been there before. Nor had he ever traveled to California. He only knew from his new employer's brochure that Downey was a part of the greater Los Angeles area and that it was far away from home. Although Arkansas was not a part of the dust bowl of the dirty thirties, Perry decided to go west for better job prospects like those who inhabited the high plains in the second wave of the drought.

The money that his new job was offering was so good that he asked for an advancement. He used it to buy Lois an engagement ring. She was happy to accept when he proposed, but was leery about moving so far away from her family. Perry promised that they would travel back to Arkansas often. It was a promise that he rarely kept. He loved the calm California weather and dreaded the hot, humid Arkansas summers. He did not mind not having to deal with the destructive weather storms that plagued Arkansas because it was one of the eleven states comprising the Tornado Alley. Southern California did not have tornadoes or snow storms. The year-round milder weather did wonders for Perry. Although Lois also enjoyed the great California weather, she resented not being able to see her family and being isolated from them so far away from home. Her only comfort was a bottle of Jack Daniels, which she chugged often and every chance she could. She was always drunk before three o'clock and would rarely come outside. Their three adult children, Matthew, Carol, and David, never visited California. They had all moved back one after the other to attend the University of Arkansas so that they could live closer to Lois's family. That only made Lois drink more.

Perry did not mind that Lois was an alcoholic. That only meant that he did not have to hear her complaining all day. He could fiddle in his workshop all day and then he could listen to his CB radio at night because she would fall asleep no later than seven o'clock every day. He reveled in hearing truckers announce where they were and where they were going or what handle they used. There was Long John who hauled gear all the way from South Dakota and Peggy Sue, the only female trucker that Perry heard on the CB radio. He would often imagine her, but her ruffian voice would turn him off unless he had a glass of whiskey himself. On Friday and Saturday nights, Perry would listen to a police scanner that he bought from one of his less savory friends. Perry proudly said it was the only one in the neighborhood and that it was illegal to monitor the police. He kept the police scanner a secret even from Lois. But he would tell a few people at times and invite them over to listen on occasion. Most of the time, he would listen by himself. Perry would casually listen as the police described an accident scene or the results of a welfare check. Every night he anxiously listened to the scanner in hopes that he could hear about a wild chase after bank robbers or other fleeing felons. Serious crimes were rare in those parts of Los Angeles.

Perry had lived on Chambers Lane ever since he bought his home during the first year when he moved to California in 1935. He knew everyone on the block really well except the Mendoza family. The Mendoza family had recently purchased their home from the Smiths who decided to sell shortly after more people of color moved into the neighborhood. His best friend was Rusty, a roly-poly elder gentleman whose belly was extremely and protrudingly round. Rusty was very proud of his huge belly. Rusty often lift his shirt in front of people and rub his bare and hairy belly and say how he paid for his belly with every can of Miller beer that he drank. It was as if his belly was his mistress and he cherished his infidelity. Rusty lived across the street from Perry and rented the converted garage from the Russells. The Russells hired Rusty to operate one of their tree shredders for their tree trimming business. Rusty was always yelling across Chambers Lane at Perry for some strange, unknown reason that seemed to matter to only him. Rusty would sometimes cross the street so that Perry could hear him. But Rusty would never enter Perry's yard or his house because Lois would not allow him. Lois considered Rusty a bad influence on Perry because Rusty was single in his 60's and he never took care of his only daughter from a high school fling that he never married. Lois saw Rusty as the reason why Perry became a womanizer years ago. Lois did not really mind because she no longer wanted Perry touching her. It was also one of the reasons why she drank so much. Perry did not want to have sex with a woman who would lay on a bed lifeless like a stuffed animal. His frustration with her lack of sexual desire was immense. Not as immense, however, as her hatred for his womanizing which was only based on the fact that Perry flaunted it to everyone, especially Lois. Perry was not discrete about it like she preferred. Her reputation was sullied by his womanizing. Although strangely enough, she did not consider her constant state of inebriation as a sullying of her reputation.

On this day, Daniel knew that as he walked up the driveway, Lois would already be asleep. He could hear Rusty shouting unintelligibly across the street, but Daniel ignored him as usual and continued walking. Lucia wanted Daniel to borrow a shovel and a rake from Perry so that she could start a garden in the rear of side yard closest to the boundary of Perry's house. Perry told Lucia that that spot in her yard was the best place to plant a garden and that he would help her start it. Over the past year, Perry had given the Mendozas various fruits and vegetables from his own garden. Perry's garden was situated behind his garage, far from view of any of his neighbors or passerbys who strolled along Chambers Lane. Perry had given the Mendozas a bucket full of green beans from his latest summer crop. Lucia made smothered green beans with bacon from a recipe that she got from a co-worker. The kids loved it. She made stuffed zucchini and also stuffed bell peppers when Perry also gave her those vegetables. But she really enjoyed the home grown tomatoes, chili peppers, and the fresh strawberries. Perry promised to give her a sunflower plant from the rows of them that he grew every summer so that Lucia could plant it in her own garden. It was a fresh snack that the kids could enjoy without any of the salt that came from packaged sunflower seeds like Davids. With all the extra food that she was able to cook without having to purchase from a grocery store, Lucia decided that she would plant her own garden. She could then avoid the awkward feeling when receiving vegetables from Perry and Lois. However, Lucia had no experience with a garden and did not have any tools to plant one. So she asked Daniel to borrow them from Perry earlier that day.

He waited until later in the day because Daniel dreaded having to borrow anything from Perry. Perry was the proverbial dirty old man who flaunted that every chance he could even with the neighborhood kids. Daniel tried to avoid any contact with him, but felt ashamed telling his mother how Perry was. Daniel suspected that it would not matter if he told his mother about Perry's antics. She would force him to go there anyway. So Daniel cautiously proceeded up the driveway towards the detached garage. He was leery of what Perry would do or say that late afternoon.

As he entered the garage, Daniel could see several girlie magazines strewn throughout the garage. Because Lois never came inside the garage, Perry felt free to leave then out in the open. He could care less if anyone saw them. It was Perry's garage and, if anyone entered, it was because they wanted something from him and not the other way around. That person would have to deal with Perry's idiosyncrasies if they wanted Perry's assistance, even if they were distasteful to most people.

"Hi Perry. My mom wanted me to ask you a favor." Daniel could tell that Perry had not heard him because Perry was still slowly grinding burrs from the aluminum pipe. "HEY PERRY!!" Daniel said with an even louder voice without trying to shout, but he needed to be heard over the belt sander.

Perry looked to his left and could see Daniel standing awkwardly near the garage door. He turned off the belt sander, held the pipe in his left hand, and walked towards Daniel.

"This here is a fine specimen." Perry handed it to Daniel so that he could examine it for himself. Daniel could immediately tell that the pipe was a lot lighter than any of the other ones that Perry had worked on.

"Wow, this is the best one yet." Daniel was not really interested in any of the projects that Perry worked on. He had to do this dance with Perry every time his mother asked him to borrow something from Perry. Daniel handed the pipe back.

"Good, good." Perry raised the pipe to his eye level and carefully looked through it to ensure that all of the burrs were grinded off. "So what does Lucia want now?"

"She just needs a shovel and a rake."

"So she's finally going to do it. Good for her. She should have started that garden once she bought that property." Perry walked to the far back corner of his garage and grabbed both items and then gave them to Daniel. Perry went back to working on his contraption and ignored Daniel.

"Thanks, Perry."

Daniel walked out of the garage and headed home. He was glad that the interaction with Perry was quick and uneventful. He was worried that Perry would grab one of the girlie magazines and insist on showing it to Daniel like he had done previously. Those were the type of antics that Perry typically would do when anyone visited him in the garage. He would proceed to talk about his heyday and how many women he had over the years. He would also talk about the neighborhood married women that he claimed to have trysts with. His bravado was unbecoming, but Perry never seemed to care. Daniel never cared for this and never cared for Perry. He could not understand why an adult male would act like this to children. No one in the neighborhood seemed to care. So long as Perry gave his vegetables and his time to help the other neighbors, they all turned a blind eye to him.

Chapter Nine

# Graduation Day

The humongous black chalkboard consumed almost the entire western wall of Mr. Morrison's math class. He would occasionally use this chalkboard to instruct his students who signed up to learn algebra, geometry, trigonometry, calculus, or physics when they especially had difficulty understanding a particular topic. All four grades of Lynwood High School students could sign up for any of those courses at any hour of the day. This flexibility was convenient for students because verbal classroom instructions by Mr. Morrison was not the main method that he used to teach students who signed up for his math lab. Instead, each of the students would check out a cassette player and a cassette tape of a lecture with that week's assignment on it. The student was also given an accompanying three-inch loose-leaf binder with hand drawn illustrations of various math problems and solutions for that assignment. Mr. Morrison's voice excitedly narrated the lecture on each cassette tape. Students could easily follow along while reading the contents of the binder; flipping the laminated illustrated pages along the three steel rings that bound it as the lecture continued. Students would listen to the lecture with headphones on so as not to disturb other students. They could listen at their leisure and rewind the tape as often as they liked to hear Mr. Morrison explain a topic again and again. When stuck, the student could ask a lab assistant to explain in detail the mathematical concepts. Sometimes, a lab assistant was a student from a higher grade, but oftentimes they were a volunteer college student or a full-time teacher's assistant. The explanations by these lab assistants would help that student overcome a personal hurdle that hindered them from comprehending the concept and finishing the assignment. When Mr. Morrison learned of a particular concept that an entire class was struggling with, then he would get the entire class's attention and explain it himself on the chalkboard; stopping at times to answer a question or two. He also would give individual attention to those students whom he knew struggled with math in general.

But on this day, the entire chalkboard was filled with bold block letters that were obviously not Mr. Morrison's handwriting, which most students knew could be illegible at times. When the third period class entered the math lab, each of the students could easily see the white chalk lines making out the words: "CONGRATULATIONS!!! CLASS OF 1983." Mr. Morrison decided to have a celebration for the graduating senior class and all the other students whom he taught, regardless of grade, were invited to attend. Ten purple and gold trophies were lined up on a table near the chalkboard. Another round table at the back of the classroom had a cake, chips, soda, and party favors for the celebration. Some music in honor of Van Halen's recent Memorial Day concert was playing in the background. When seniors Antonio Vega, Oscar Prado, and Richard Kunkle finally entered the classroom, other students clapped. Veronica Shin and Daniel Mendoza were already in the classroom sitting next to Cheryl Westerbrooke and Gloria Martinez. They were the main seniors graduating that year from Mr. Morrison's third period class. Seniors Brenda Montana, Georgette McNichols, and Monica Williams from the fifth period class also attended the party.

"Hey everyone. I finally have some good news." Mr. Morrison grinned from ear to ear as he announced this while standing in front of the chalkboard. "Our star pupil, Daniel Mendoza, who as you can see on our leader board, is top in geometry (which he finished in one semester), top in trigonometry, calculus, and physics." This was not anything new to any of the students listening. They had heard Mr. Morrison brag about Daniel Mendoza every semester. Mr. Morrison then pointed to the cork board adjacent to the chalkboard that was covered in purple construction paper and outlined with gold. "Today's 'Knight City Knews' is that Mr. Mendoza is also the class of 1983's valedictorian! Also give a round of applause to Ms. Shin, who is salutatorian." Daniel's name along with Veronica Shin's name were written on white construction paper that was pinned to the cork board. The room again filled with applause. Mr. Morrison handed a trophy to both Daniel and Veronica when they approached the front of the classroom. Mr. Morrison handed out the remaining trophies and also certificates to other students.

When he was finished, Daniel Mendoza stood up and walked to the front of the class and spoke; his long, gangly appendages gesticulated wildly as he did so. "We've all been in Mr. Morrison's class these past four years, at least those of us in the class of 1983. Being in Mr. Morrison's classes has taught us a lot. He means a lot to me as a teacher and a mentor and he has encouraged each and every one of us to do well in school, to finish our modules and homework and, of course, apply to college. He has been a mentor to me and I know too many of you. The class of 1983 wanted to do something nice for Mr. Morrison. Gabriel…"

Daniel stood aside and began clapping as Gabriel Ramirez carried in a four-foot tall, purple and gold trophy engraved with "Mr. Morrison. World's Greatest Math Teacher." Mr. Morrison reached out to shake Gabriel's hand and then took the trophy from Gabriel and held it up with both hands. His eyes began to tear up.

"Thank you. Thank you all." He wiped his tears and tried to continue, but he choked up again. The class continued clapping and everyone stood up.

"It's alright Mr. Morrison," Daniel came up to Mr. Morrison and put his arm around him.

The party continued until the end of the fourth period. Only Daniel and Veronica lingered after the party. Daniel was working on his valedictory speech and looked up when he sensed that Veronica was needlessly hanging around the math lab with no apparent purpose. He watched her walk haphazardly around the room as if she was pacing and had something on her mind. He was going to ask her if she was okay, but he knew that Veronica would not speak unless she was ready to. So Daniel held back his tongue and continued making last minute revisions to his valedictory speech.

Veronica stopped pacing and said aloud as if speaking to herself, "This doesn't make any sense. It doesn't." Daniel looked up again and watched her more attentively. He wondered what did not make any sense, but had no idea. Veronica continued pacing even more frantically than before. She would have worn out the tile flooring had she not stopped pacing when she turned abruptly around towards Daniel.

"You aren't supposed to be valedictorian," she blurted out finally.

Daniel was astonished and a sense of anger or frustration began to slowly bubble up inside of him. He tried to restrain it so that he could hear Veronica out. "What do you mean?" he asked.

"I'm supposed to be valedictorian. Every Shin in my family has graduated as valedictorian of Lynwood High School. My older brother, Alex, was valedictorian for the class of 1979 and Kayla was valedictorian in 1981. Because I'm not graduating as valedictorian, I know my father will be very disappointed. I have failed the family." She had apparently not told her family.

Daniel wondered why this was so important to Veronica. It was well known that her family owned the McDonald's on Atlantic Avenue and that Kayla worked there as a night manager. In Daniel's mind, that was not a big accomplishment. He wondered, after attending UCLA with him, would Veronica graduate and then go work for her parents at their McDonald's. Daniel planned on getting an aerospace engineering degree and planned on working for Hughes Aircraft or Lockheed or Boeing. He was puzzled why it mattered to Veronica whether she graduated first or second in their class because, no matter what, she already had a job. It did not really matter if she went to college or not.

Daniel wanted to make a smart remark about how he has been first in every honors and AP class that they took together, that he received the highest grade in every assignment and every test, that he worked very hard in every class and, on top of all this, also worked twenty to thirty hours after school as a clerk at Montgomery Wards during his junior and senior years. But he knew that anything he said to vindicate himself would not make any difference to Veronica. He did not want to start an argument on the last day of class, especially because it was graduation day. He wondered what his mentor, Mr. Morrison, would have advised him to say in this moment. He drew upon everything that Mr. Morrison had told him over the years before speaking.

"Veronica, you've done a fantastic job in high school. You've been accepted to UCLA, and are in the top two of your class. I'm sure your parents will be very proud of you and, in the end, it really won't matter."

Veronica paused and took a deep sigh. "Do you really think so?" she asked.

Having never met her parents over the past six years that he knew her since Hosler Junior High School, Daniel could only guess whether her parents would respond this way. He was too young to know about Tiger Moms or other ways that Asian students like Veronica felt pressured to succeed that other students did not. He never felt such pressures at home himself. His mother, Lucia, was apathetic towards Daniel's success in school. She rarely attended any of his award ceremonies over the years and was disinterested when he told her that he was accepted into UCLA. In fact, she asked Daniel why he even needed to go to college. His mother told him that he could stay home and live with her and pay her rent the way that Maria and Jose Luis did when they turned eighteen. Neither of them had graduated from high school or attended any community college. Daniel thought that his mother would be proud of him to be the first in the family to graduate and be accepted into college. It was something that motivated him secretly over the years. He was surprised and extremely disappointed when she discouraged him from attending college.

Daniel Mendoza knew since he was in the second grade that he wanted to attend college. He had been in the PACE (Program for Accelerated and Clustered Education) program since attending Magnolia Elementary School. The PACE program placed Daniel together with other highly capable students in his grade level in the same part of the classroom and taught these PACE students core curricula above his grade. The other students in the class were only taught the general education for that grade. The PACE program gave Daniel a sense of direction and a strong need to accomplish more than his peers, including his siblings who were never a part of the program. Every student in the program was expected to attend college. It was a given and never posed as a desire. By the time he was in the sixth grade, Daniel knew that he wanted to attend UCLA. It was the only college that he applied to when he was a senior. He knew that if he graduated as valedictorian, then he had an excellent chance to get accepted into UCLA. Daniel also knew that if he was valedictorian then he could qualify for a full scholarship sponsored by Hughes Aircraft. However, he would need to select aerospace engineering as his major. For years, this was Daniel goal, but he never shared it with anyone including his mother.

With a longstanding desire to attend college, Daniel had ignored his mother's comments and became even more resolved to go to UCLA. He no longer wanted to live at home. His domineering mother was too oppressive and controlling. His older sister, Maria, was the same way. It only made living at home even more unbearable. Jose Luis, with his immature and aggressive attitude, was no better. Daniel would finally be free and on his own, yet unaware of what perils and adventures were awaiting him.

Daniel was even more perplexed when Veronica told him that she would not be moving into the dorms with him and Gabriel, who had also been accepted to UCLA. Her parents wanted Veronica to live at home and commute to school every day. It was a forty-five minute drive each way in LA traffic. Daniel wondered if this was a form of punishment because Veronica was salutatorian and not valedictorian. He also wondered whether it added to Veronica's angst that day. He tried to get those thoughts out of his mind and focus on encouraging her instead. When he sensed that she had calmed down, he inquired about the graduation ceremony that night and whether she had received five tickets like all of the other graduating seniors. Veronica reminded him that all of the top ten students received an extra pair of tickets as a reward. Daniel had completely forgotten about the extra tickets. He was unsure whether his siblings would attend, let alone his mother. He knew that he had no need for seven tickets and that five was more than enough. He left the tickets on the television console that morning in plain sight because he would not have time to go home before the graduation ceremony. Daniel thought about giving his extra tickets to Veronica, but knew it was impossible because he did not have them on him.

Veronica thanked Daniel again for encouraging her, exited the math lab, and went home to get ready for the graduation ceremony; leaving Daniel alone in the math lab. He continued revising his graduation speech and then changed into a grey, pinned-striped suit that he bought at Wards for his graduation. Daniel then put on the white graduation gown, which he knew would stand out. All of the male students wore purple gowns and the women wore gold gowns in honor of the school colors. Daniel and Veronica both had white gowns. He then placed the baby blue National Honor Society stole around his neck and ensured that it laid properly so that the emblem was centered over his heart. Once it was, he placed the gold honors cords around his neck and then the white cap on his head, gathered his valedictory speech into a manilla folder, and walked towards the football field where the graduation ceremony would be held in the next thirty minutes.

When he arrived near the entrance of the football field, Daniel was told to walk to the front of the line where Monica Williams, Cheryl Westerbrooke, and Robert Kunkle were already waiting. Veronica was in the front of another line and the students were alternatively placed in the two lines depending on their last name. As Pomp and Circumstance played, they all walked into the stadium and could see Julian Bond and the other dignitaries, including Principal Gina Westmoreland and School Superintendent Helena Moss, sitting on an elevated, ceremonial platform with some of the other teachers including Mr. Morrison. The students sat in metal chairs on each side of the platform and the top ten students sat in front of the platform.

After Daniel sat down, he scanned the bleachers to see if his mother and siblings had arrived. The other students and the commotion of parents and guests arriving at the ceremony distracted him from his efforts. Soon the ceremony began with a benediction and then after a while it was Daniel's turn to give his speech. He walked up to the podium and proceeded:

Education. Tonight, we are honoring education. For the past few years, this graduating class has gone through hundreds of tests, several term papers, and Mr. McCann. We've done it all and we have seen it all. We worked on chemistry, calculus, physics, and biology. A few of us have stayed long hours into the night either to read books or finish our homework. If you walked down the corridors of the B-Building, you could see students frantically rushing to read their cliff notes and write their Kempersition...

By the end of the speech, Daniel found his older sister, Maria, and his younger sister, Sylvia, sitting alone near the top right of the bleachers. He gave them a smile and waved and walked to his chair and sat down. He realized, however, that neither his mother nor his brother, Jose Luis, were there. Although that disappointed him, he reassured himself that it was to be expected.

Chapter Ten

# Marriage Proposal

The many bronze mini-chandeliers lit up the long herringbone brick walkway so that the arches reflected the light downward and then outward past the Romanesque columns supporting it. The light then emulated into the grassy courtyard between Powell Library and Royce Hall where a few straggling students began packing up their books and walking home. Daniel Mendoza glanced over towards them as he casually strolled the walkway with his overstuffed, dark leather Jansport backpack tightly gripped so that it did not weigh down his back as he walked. He had recently left the University Research Library because it closed at 11 p.m. He had been studying alone that evening for his thermodynamics and materials engineering finals, which were almost two weeks away. Having first walked passed Rolfe Hall and Campbell Hall, Daniel had previously turned right to walk underneath this arched walkway of Royce Hall. Royce Hall's brick and tile exterior enclosed a large concert auditorium which could not be seen by visitors in the courtyard. Such visitors could only see the iconic twin-towered facade that was symbolic of UCLA and known internationally. Royce Hall had once been the main classroom at UCLA when the campus was small and new. As Daniel walked that evening, he was not thinking about the two music classes that he had at Royce Hall when he was a sophomore and a junior, or the many times he performed at Spring Sing there with his fraternity, or the various concerts held inside especially those that were held prior to his attendance by Frank Sinatra, Elle Fitzgerald, Leonard Bernstein, the New York Philharmonic, and many notable others. Instead, as he took the long walk back to his fraternity house on Landfair Avenue, Daniel's mind was contemplating his future now that he was finally graduating with an aerospace engineering degree.

He was excited and yet afraid of the future. A part of him wanted to meander home that night, but he knew that the fraternity had a celebration the following evening. So Daniel continued determinedly, but slowly home. He stopped when he reached the top of Janss Steps. As a graduating senior, he had just pledged a thousand dollars to his senior class gift. The senior gift which was a water fountain just east of where he was standing at the entrance of the courtyard. He turned around to look at the proposed spot and wondered how the fountain would look. He had recently seen the plans, but he realized that he might never see it built. Daniel thought it would be a great gift that future students would enjoy just like he had enjoyed the inverted fountain near Kinsey Hall all these years. When Daniel turned back around towards Janss steps, he admired the view. From the top of Janss steps, he could see Drake stadium and behind that, further in the distance, was Sproul Hall. Sproul Hall was the dormitory where Daniel lived his freshman year before joining his fraternity. The newer Dykstra Hall was to its left. Daniel remembered that Gabriel's freshman dorm room was in Dykstra Hall. He wondered what happened to Gabriel. They had not seen each other since their sophomore year when Gabriel dropped out of UCLA to marry a Venezuelan girl. Gabriel met her on campus in one of his science classes. Daniel learned that Gabriel married after he found out that she was pregnant. Had the years been kind to them? Were they still together? Or did

Gabriel leave her the same way his father did? Daniel would never know.

Daniel shook off these thoughts and continued walking down the exterior 87 steps, which were once the main entrance to the original campus. As he neared the bottom of the stairs, he ensured that he hopped over the sixth step from the bottom. It was a silly habit that he developed after touring the campus as a high school senior. Daniel learned from the UCLA student who was his tour guide that one of the Janss brothers, who has sold the land to UCLA, was supposedly buried beneath the sixth step. It was bad luck for anyone to step on it. Daniel never really believed it. During this his senior year, Daniel wondered if freshman students were even told about the legend anymore. When he gave campus tours over the years, Daniel always told the story of the Janss brothers. But as is natural of aging young adults, skepticism had crept in and the vigor and eagerness of youth slowly faded. When Daniel reached the bottom of Janss steps, he noticed an older gentleman approaching near the lamppost that illuminated the right side of the bottom steps.

"How are you doing this evening, Daniel? Were your studies productive?" The familiar voice was Daniel's father. He would occasionally meet his father at this location especially on nights like this when Daniel studied alone and not with any of his fraternity brothers or pledges. As pledge master, Daniel would have to study with the pledges every Thursday night because it was a mandatory study night. Because it was nearing finals, those mandatory study times were on hiatus until the next quarter when a new set of pledges were inducted.

"I'm doing alright," Daniel hesitantly answered.

"You don't sound like it. What's on your mind?"

Daniel was reluctant to discuss it, but he knew that his father would figure it out after a short while. Pretending nothing was bothering him was futile. Daniel took a step forward and continued talking, hoping that his father would follow him. They walked left towards Bruin Walk and along the path past the student activities center; the pool was silent and still at this time of night.

"I have a job offer at Rockwell International in the Space Shuttle Main Engine Program, but I don't think that I am going to take it." Daniel knew that his father would not ask why, but was strategically patient and would wait until Daniel volunteered the information. They continued walking in silence for a few seconds until he did. "I also applied to various law schools, but the only one that I was accepted into is the University of San Diego. It's a small campus. It's not a prestigious school and is ranked low, but at least I can study law."

Daniel explained that, although he had an aptitude for engineering, the work was mundane and really just a lot of paper work. He had imagined designing things like the hypersonic plane or a manned expedition to Mars (which was the topic of his senior paper). The design phase of such programs lasted no more than a decade and the production stage would typical likely last 20 to 30 years or more. So any role that Daniel could have as an aerospace engineer would be limited to resolving any problems with the Space Shuttle main engine. He would never be able to contribute to designing it. Daniel had learned from an older engineer that worked at Rocketdyne that, to do any actually designing, Daniel would need a Ph.D. Getting a Ph.D. in engineering would take six years or more of graduate studies. Daniel was unsure of whether he wanted to spend that amount of time studying engineering. He was not in love with it anymore like he was when he studied physics and calculus in Mr. Morrison's classes in high school.

"Are there any other ways that you can use your engineering degree at Rockwell?" His dad asked.

"I can hope to become a project manager someday. But I would eventually need to earn an MBA and then I wouldn't be doing engineering anymore. I would be pushing paper. I guess if my future is to push paper, why shouldn't I just become an attorney anyway?" Daniel knew what his father would say, but he awaited a response.

They turned right onto Bruin Walk and headed towards the John Wooden Center and continued talking.

"What's keeping you from going to law school?"

"Nothing really." He hesitated and then continued, "Well, that's not true. There is someone special in my life."

"Is there?" Daniel's father said with a gleaming smile.

Daniel proceeded to tell his father about Christina Bradley and how he meet her at the UCLA law library when he was studying there one day. She was studying their too because she was a law student at UCLA. Daniel explained that Christina was two years Daniel's senior and would be graduating from the law school the following year. Daniel was thinking of marrying her. He was concerned that moving away to San Diego for law school may hurt their two year relationship.

"She is wonderful, Dad. She can be stubborn at times, but she challenges me. I like that about her. She is bright and intelligent and she is always laughing and enjoying herself despite all of the things that she has been through in her life. I really care deeply for her."

"But what is your concern then?"

When Daniel reached the bronze Bruin Bear statue near the center of Bruin plaza, he sat down on the large marble, rectangular pedestal near the bear's front left paw. His father also sat down closer to the right paw, which was poised in a walking position a little behind the left front leg. They sat watching the few students who remained walk back to their dorms. The students continued walking straight to the right of the statue. Many of those students lived in a frat house or in apartments on Gayley or Landfair. They had to turn left around the statue and walk past Pauley Pavilion. After all the students walked passed or around the Bruin Bear and they were alone, Daniel continued.

"I'm embarrassed to say. Actually, I feel guilty. She has a three year old son, Wisdom. He is adorable. I love him so and I think he loves me too."

"There's nothing wrong with feeling guilty about that. Kids are a wonderful thing. Are you concerned that Wisdom isn't yours?"

"That's not it. I'm more concerned about Christina. She … She isn't always trusting. She was hurt really bad by Wisdom's father. He was very abusive toward her, stole her inheritance, cheated on her and got another woman pregnant. She loves me. I know it, but she is not willing to open up like she should and doesn't trust her judgment about men, including me."

Daniel stood up and began pacing around the statue. His head faced down as he walked in an undesigned and chaotic path. His father watched as Daniel paced. The steps eventually shortened until Daniel was at rest and facing the statue. Daniel looked directly at his father's face for comfort.

"Son, sit down." Daniel complied. "It will all work out. Try not to worry about it. You just need to ask yourself if you really do love Christina."

Daniel pondered for a moment and then let out a deep sigh. "I do love her, Dad. I really do. I think about her all the time. She is my first thought every morning and my last thought every night. I want to do what is best for her and Wisdom. I want to be a better man for them. I want to take care of them. When I tell Christina that she smiles. I see it in her eyes as well. She's trying to trust me and open up, but there's always something gnawing in the back of her mind. She hasn't let her past go yet. Maybe I'm asking too much from her?"

"Does that effect how you feel about her?"

"No, it doesn't. I still love her. I can't explain it."

"If you love her, Daniel, then you should marry her. Don't let the doubts and fears control you. If you do, then you will miss out on love and you'll never know when it comes again. It may never. Trust in yourself and in Christina. If you both are willing to work at your relationship, then it will work out. You'll see."

Daniel realized that his father was right and that he should trust in their love. He should do what makes him happy and what makes Christina happy. He realized that marrying her would make him happy. He could be happier than he had ever been in years, especially after that dark day years ago at Ramona Elementary School when he saw Marcelo in the MG with another woman. He deserved happiness and so did Christina. That thought brought Daniel a sense of relief.

"Hey, you there." An older gentleman in his late thirties approached the Bruin Bear statue. His black buttoned shirt contained a blue and gold badge with the words "UCLA Campus Security."

Daniel looked to his right towards the officer. "Yes, officer. Is there anything that you need?"

The officer took a few steps closer and said, "It's getting late and you shouldn't be outside by yourself."

Daniel looked around the marble pedestal and noticed only his Jansport backpack on it. No one else was around other than the campus security officer. Daniel grabbed the backpack, put it on, and responded, "Sorry officer. I'll be going."

Daniel stood up, walked around the statue, and began walking towards Pauley Pavilion alone.

Chapter Eleven

# Private Eye

The wooden shutters were slightly opened allowing just a little of the summer morning sun to enter into Daniel's office on
the east side of the fifteenth floor of the Dial Building. The sun
slightly blinded him when he looked out that window as he
faced his computer armoire trying to work. He could still see
the well-known contours of Camelback Mountain; whose shape
resembled that of a kneeling camel. If Daniel looked closely,
he could make out the camel's hump protruding massively on
the horizon. The smaller, more-jagged sandstone mountain that
formed the camel's head appeared to be eerily looking in his direction. It was as if the camel was greeting him each and every
workday. As Daniel gazed at the mountain, he could make out
a few of the million dollar homes that dotted its base. He pondered how it would be like to live in such homes in the richer
Arcadia neighborhood of Phoenix, Arizona. Daniel wondered if
he owned a home there whether he would also hike the various
trails or go rock climbing like many of its neighbors did. As a
senior associate at his law firm, Daniel knew that he could not
yet afford an expensive house. One or two of the partners at
his firm lived in that neighborhood. It was not anything that he
strongly desired anyway.

So Daniel continued working letting his mind encapsulate and absorb all of the information contained in the documents that he skimmed on his computer screen. He needed to review over one thousand pages of documents from a construction defect case that he had been working on. Earlier that morning, he read the various pleadings: the complaint and answer and the subsequent two amended complaints with their corresponding answers filed by the defendants, a general contractor and the husband and wife owners. He had learned that the general contractor had allegedly misdirected the plaintiffs' monies to other projects that the contractor had. It was alleged that the general contractor possibly diverted the plaintiffs' monies to other business enterprises, leaving the plaintiffs with an unfinished custom home. The home had no garage doors or flooring or kitchen cabinets. Other items were missing because the contractor refused to complete the job unless the plaintiffs, Mr. and Mrs. Savard, issued another check for past work performed. Daniel was desperately looking for a document indicating where the money had gone and whether the allegations were true. He finally came across a criminal indictment accusing the general contractor's accountant of absconding with over two hundred thousand dollars. The accountant apparently used the monies for her gambling addiction.

Daniel needed to locate this woman so that she could testify that she indeed stole the money from her employer. Perhaps her willingness to accept criminal blame and accept a six month prison sentence meant that the accountant had changed her ways and would be willing to testify about her actions in the insurance coverage lawsuit that Daniel had been working on these past few months. He quickly skimmed though the documents, but could not find her contact information. Unable to call the female accountant, Daniel instead called Pamela White with Investigators United.

"Good morning, this is Joanne with Investigators United. How can I help you?"

"My name is Daniel Mendoza. I'm an attorney with the law firm of Williams Brown. I was hoping to speak with Pamela White. I have a new case that I would like to hire her for."

"Could you hold please?"

Daniel waited until a young, excited voice answered the phone. He instantly recognized the voice as Pamela's because Daniel had utilized her service once before in a class action lawsuit involving improper fax transmissions.

"Pamela White speaking," the voice said.

"Hey, Pamela. It's Daniel Mendoza. Remember, you helped me on the Ramsey Radiator case."

"That's been a long time. I remember that case. Thanks for remembering me."

Daniel was used to this typical meet and greet routine anytime he needed an outside vendor to accomplish a task that his firm did not have the resources to do. Locating an individual was something that he may have had one of the paralegals do, but Daniel was keenly aware that he had a limited amount of time to locate the accountant. Pamela was great with such fast turn-around tasks. He proceeded to explain to her the misappropriation of the Savards' money by the general contractor, the accountant's gambling addiction, and her subsequent criminal indictment and imprisonment. They continued discussing the case until the conversation came to a natural end when Pamela interjected that she wanted to get more of his firm's investigative work.

"I want to show you that I can accomplish any task. Let me do something for you for free. Anything you want."

Daniel pondered for a moment about what particular task that he wanted to give Pamela to prove her investigatory skills. He quickly thought of his many lawsuits to figure out which ones may need an investigator. Nothing stuck out. But then it dawned on him. He always wanted to find his father. His mother, Lucia, divorced Jose Luis Mendoza, Senior when Daniel was not even one years old. Daniel had never met his father and seeing him for the first time after all these years would be welcomed. Daniel envisioned calling his father, hearing his voice, and explaining that he was his son. He hoped that it would lead to more talks and then perhaps a visit to New York. Daniel knew that his father lived on Long Island, but did not know where that was or what it meant. Was his father well off? Did he remarry? Did he have more kids? Did he ever look for Daniel and his other siblings? Or was his father obstinate and did he refused to even acknowledge that he even had kids? Daniel wondered about all of these things and, at the same time, was fearful of knowing the answers.

With little information about his father, Daniel told Pamela that he wanted her to locate him. He gave her his father's full name, that he lived in New York (although Daniel was unsure whether his father still lived there), and his approximate age. Pamela acknowledged that this was little to go on, but she was up to the challenge. She wanted to prove to Daniel that she was an excellent investigator so she agreed.

Two weeks later, Daniel received a call from Pamela asking for more information. "If I had his birthday or social security number, I could really narrow it down. Your father's name is very popular in New York. And I'm not sure if he is any of the forty-two men in New York that I located." Daniel could sense a little frustration in Pamela's voice.

"Pam, I really do appreciate all that you've done for me so far. The only thing that I can do is ask my mom whether she has any more information." Daniel was aware that his mother rarely talked about his father. He also knew that it would be a struggle to get any more information out of her.

"When you do, just let me know and I can continue with the research. I really do want to help you locate your father."

Pamela hung up the phone leaving Daniel pondering what he could do or say to his mother to extract any additional information from her. He wondered whether he should call Maria and ask her to get the information from their mother. He knew Maria always wanted to find their father, but Daniel did not want Maria to get the credit for finding him. So he decided against it. He would figure it out himself without Maria's help.

A few days passed and then a week. Daniel allowed his long work days and lazy nights to distract him from calling his mother. He had not heard back from Pamela so he thought about letting it all go. Why fret over someone he really did not know and who probably did not care to know him? But a nagging desire haunted him. Daniel knew that he would regret losing this opportunity to locate his father so he had to do what anyone would do under the circumstances and call his mother no matter the result. It was his only hope of getting enough information to locate his father.

Daniel grabbed his iPhone, opened the contacts app, located his mother's contact info, and saw her picture. He envisioned hearing her voice answering the phone.

"Hey mijo, what are you doing?" His mother's voice was surprisingly pleasant which made him pause initially and doubt whether it was truly her.

"I'm just relaxing." Daniel rarely spoke to his mother so the first few minutes were always awkward. The awkwardness was the reason why he did not call her as often as his other siblings. But he struggled to press through it so that he could try to find his father.

"How's work? Are you working on any exciting cases?"

Daniel knew that his mother would always ask about his job. No matter how many times he explained it, she never really understood what he did for a living, only that he was an attorney. She would offer to pray for him and pray that he would get his own clients, whatever that meant. But he obliged as he always did. They chatted for a while about his law firm and the partners and the new cases that he was assigned to. When the conversation reached the retention of a private investigator for his new case with the Savards, Daniel used that opportunity to let his mother know that Pamela offered to locate his father for free.

"Yes, mom. She said free. I think that was nice of her. Don't you? She normally charges $75 per hour."

"I really don't know anything. Your father and I were married only three years. Just enough time to have the three of you." Daniel could sense the nervousness in his mother's voice.

"You have to know something, mom. Anything. You never celebrated his birthday?"

"I know it was in October, but I don't remember the day. It's been a long time. I have bad memories with your dad so I try to forget all that."

Daniel was hesitant to press further because he did not want to hurt his mother in any way. But this was important and he had to get the information to give to Pamela. So he continued asking about his father.

"Do you know what year he was born?"

"No, but I think that he was two years younger than me."

Daniel knew that his mother was born in 1945 so he figured that his father may have been born sometime in 1947. It was just a guess. It was the first time Daniel learned that his father was actually younger than his mother. He had always thought that his father was several years older, which would have been typical at that time. Even this fact brought some encouragement. Why did his mother marry a younger man when she was a child herself? Why would his father marry an "older" woman? Was this a source of tension between them and were they ostracized by society? Daniel realized that his mother may be inaccurate about the age difference, but at least it would be something to give Pamela that she could use. He then pressed his mother for his father's social security number, but she insisted that she did not know it.

"I don't understand. I remember that you used to get child support from our father for a couple of years when I was a teenager. How could you get child support without having his social security number?"

Lucia did not respond.

Daniel was frustrated with the lack of information that his mother had. He had many more personal questions about his father that he wanted to ask, but never learned over the years. Besides his father's name, Daniel knew little about him. What was even more frustrating was that his mother never really expected that her children would want to meet their father. She never prepared for this day. One would have expected that the Mendoza children would have asked much sooner about their father. None of them did. Daniel was in his forties when he first started asking his mother about his father. As Daniel contemplated this, he realized that his mother never encouraged him or his siblings to find their father when they were children or even when they were young adults. Perhaps, she never wanted them to find him and was now refusing to be helpful to discourage Daniel from trying. Was she afraid that her older children would build a closer relationship with their father? It was not as if she had a close relationship with her children. Was she afraid that he would reveal things about their marriage that she did not want her children to know that could undermine what little she had told them? Daniel's thoughts swirled as to why his mother was so apathetic towards his desire to meet his father. Daniel, however, did not let this effect his enthusiasm, but he could not help but feel like it was now somewhat dulled and restrained.

By the following day, there was still a sense of hopefulness. So Daniel called Pamela and gave her the limited new information that he could glean from his mother. With that, Pamela narrowed the list to three men who could potentially be Daniel's father. She emailed the list of prospects to Daniel and then called him at home later that evening.

"I have good news and bad news," she added with a slight hesitation. "This is the best that I can do without more specifics."

"I know you're doing your best. I can't wait to find out."

"Well, the gentlemen that I think is your father lived on Long Island just like you told me. The bad news is that, based on what I learned, he passed away two years ago." Daniel was silent. "I know this is disappointing, but there are two other men who could also be your dad. I just can't make a definitive decision without your father's actual birthdate or social security."

"So there is a possibility that the other two can be my father."

"I'm not going to lie to you, Daniel. There is a possibility, but I think it's a slim possibility. I really believe that your father is the man who passed away two years ago." Pamela explained her reasons.

Daniel became dejected. His anger towards his mother increased. Why did she not keep his father's social security number and birthdate? Why was she so unwilling to talk about him? If she had, Daniel would finally have some closure after all these years. That closure continued to evade him. Daniel no longer made any effort to locate his father and had given him up for dead.

Chapter Twelve

# More Than Just One

The circular flagstone seating area was encompassed on the northwestern side by two raised flowerbed walls that were made of stone. The flowerbeds never really contained any flowers over the years. Instead, in order to save water as well as money, it was xeriscaped with over a dozen barrel cacti and several aloe vera plants and some Spanish lavender that grew two to three feet tall. The sweet scent of lavender encapsulated anyone seated there especially during the winter months in Glendale, Arizona, which were more like a warm Spring. In the middle of the seating area was a circular travertine table with a fire pit. The fire pit had a roaring fire made from many cut limbs of mesquite wood from the nearby three humongous Chilean mesquite trees that lined the western fence of the property. The trees shaded most of the backyard including the flagstone seating area where Daniel sat that early Saturday afternoon. The fire crackled and snapped. Occasionally, hummingbirds perched on the tops of the mesquite trees. The whirling of their fast-paced wings could be heard over the sound of R&B music playing from the iPad on Daniel's lap. A family of quails were haphazardly walking in the lawn looking for food for the five baby quails that quickly tagged along behind their bigger and fatter parents. Honey bees roamed around the myrtle bushes. A gecko or two scurried near the top of the fence whenever anything frightened them. The gecko would become frightened if they perceived that this big, vague figure near them was going to stand up and walk in their direction. The geckos would dart back into the sun to warm themselves when they realized that nothing was headed their way.

Daniel sat on a sunbrella-padded, swiveling chair and listened to R&B music. He was perusing his Facebook newsfeed and posting a comment or two. Daniel shared a Puerto Rican recipe from a Facebook group that he liked. The Freakin Rican Restaurant had posted a video on how to make yucca pasteles. Daniel also shared it on his niece's Facebook wall. He hoped that they could make some yucca pasteles later that year when he made his annual trek to Corona to visit Marie and her husband for Thanksgiving. He also shared pictures posted by the Puerto Rican Historic Building Society of the Cabo San Juan lighthouse in Fajardo. The lighthouse was located on a high promontory near the end of a peninsula that was isolated from the mainland because of a large lagoon and some marshes to the lighthouse's south. Daniel remembered seeing the lighthouse in the distance when he stayed at the El Conquistador Resort and Spa several years earlier. He had planned on visiting the lighthouse on that occasion, but he never made it. Last year, he had planned on returning to the resort as part of his fiftieth birthday celebration, but he was reluctant to travel alone again. He had hoped that he would be in a committed relationship by now and that the getaway would be a romantic weekend. That had not happened. He was alone. No wife and no kids. He and Christina divorced more than fifteen years ago and they never had any children together. She had sole custody of Wisdom. Daniel never saw the two again after the divorce.

Daniel believed he would have gotten married again by now, but that never panned out as well. The ensuing years were brutal and stressful; filled with long hours working at the firm and little financial reward. As he sat in the outdoor seating area listening to music, his regrets welled up inside. He tried to suppress the thoughts of what could have been or what should have been and, at times, he was successful. That afternoon, however, his mind was finally distracted when he received a text from his older sister, Maria.

"I have something to tell you", the text read mysteriously.

Daniel was surprised. He had not heard from Maria in over four months. He wondered what she had to tell him. He dreaded that it was another legal question about her divorce from Eduardo, but he decided to be positive about hearing from her. He hesitated before typing, worried that what he said might upset her again. He typed, "Hey Maria, what is it?" but did not send it immediately. He had disabled the read receipt function on his iPad so he knew that Maria would not know that he had already received her text and read it. Knowing her personality, Daniel knew that he had to respond shortly; otherwise, Maria would think that he was ignoring her. If Maria thought that Daniel was ignoring her, then he would never learn why she was texting him. His mind raced thinking how she would receive the text he just typed. He finally decided it was okay. So he sent it.

He waited patiently for her response. He could see the ellipsis in the messaging app indicating that Maria was typing a response. Daniel was relieved.

The text was delivered stating simply, "I found him." Daniel was confused.

"Who did you find?" he responded.

"...our father." The words stuck in his throat as he read them as if he had difficulty speaking them aloud to himself. He swiveled the chair nervously and stoked the fire so that it would warm his body even more.

"You found our father," he typed.

"Yes."

"How did you find him?"

Maria proceeded to explain how she just decided to research their father's name on Avvo, an online white pages. She found several entries in New York under the name Jose Luis Mendoza. She filtered out the ones that she knew were not him because Avvo provided associated persons with every entry. Maria remembered that, when they visited Lamont as children, her grandfather's name was Regino and their aunts' names were Julia and Margarita. Maria could not remember the name of their other aunt, the middle girl. Only one entry on Avvo had the names Regino Mendoza and their aunts' names associated with it. Maria figured that the entry must be their father. She saw the names Ernesto Mendoza and Lisa Mendoza also associated with the entry and remembered that those were the names of their father's children from his second marriage.

"Did you get an address and phone number for our father?" Daniel asked.

"It didn't have one," Maria responded.

Daniel wanted to call his sister, but he knew that she would not answer unless she felt like talking on the phone. He did not want to risk ending the conversation so he kept texting her. She explained searching for Ernesto and Lisa on Facebook. Maria searched many profiles until she found a profile of an Ernesto who looked like a picture of their young father which see remembered seeing in Margarita's photo album years ago.

"I wasn't sure if it was him," she texted. "But I prayed about it and decided to send him a friend request."

After a few minutes, no other texts were received. Daniel wondered whether he would receive another text from Maria. He continued listening to music and then decided to check Facebook himself. He entered "Lisa Mendoza Long Island New York" in the search engine. About a dozen profiles were returned as part of the search results. Daniel skimmed a few profiles and found a profile picture of a woman in her mid-forties holding a young five year old boy in her lap. The post indicated that the boy's name was Little Ernie.

"This has to be Lisa," Daniel thought to himself. "If I send her a friend request, she may not accept it." Daniel pondered what to do next. He decided to message her through Facebook and explain that he was her half-brother from her father's first marriage. Being honest, he thought, may elicit a response. She was a New Yorker so he fully expected that she would respond with skepticism. Daniel probably would think that the message was part of a scam if someone had sent it to him. He did not expect a response from Lisa. He continued listening to music and enjoying the nice winter weather.

Three days later, Daniel's iPhone buzzed indicating a message was received as part of the Facebook app.

"Who is this?" it read.

"It's me, Daniel," he typed. "I'm your brother. We have the same father, Jose Luis Mendoza."

"How do I know it's you?"

Daniel smiled and thought, "Typical." He typed, "Our father never liked being called Jose Luis. He preferred Joey. Our grandfather's name is Regino. He used to live in Lamont." Daniel provided other details about the Mendoza family that he did not realize that he knew, but subconsciously remembered at that moment. The details reassured Lisa.

"You have to remember that I'm a New Yorker and we're skeptical. You could be a scammer. I have to be careful. No offense."

"Lol. I thought you would think that," he responded. "That proves we are related."

The tensioned decreased with that last message. Daniel messaged, "I have a photo of our father that my sister, Maria, sent me. If you don't mind, I would like to share it with you. I just want to forewarn you that it's a picture of our father with my mother when she was pregnant."

"Sure, I don't have many pictures of our father when he was young."

Daniel sent Lisa the picture. They began exchanging other pictures of each other. Lisa sent a picture of Ernesto with his son and pictures of other relatives from her father's side. She was careful not to mention her mother or her mother's relatives out of concern for Daniel's feelings.

"I have some pictures of our father when he was a child." Lisa sent Daniel a wrinkled black and white photo of a young Jose Luis, Senior with a surprisingly happy smile that Daniel had never seen before. The other photos messaged showed a smiling Jose Luis with Lisa at her graduation and other events. Daniel wondered more about his father and inquired from Lisa about their relationship.

"We were really close. I was his baby girl and I respected him a lot," she added.

"It looked like he was very proud of you."

"I felt that he was especially proud of me after I graduated from college. I was saddened that he was unable to make it to my graduation from my master's program."

Daniel was perplexed by this response and he wondered if his fears were true. "Why was he unable to make it?" he inquired.

The two texted throughout that evening and eventually made plans to see each other that summer in New York. He also wanted to show Lisa where he grew up on Chambers Lane. Daniel was happy to finally have a family member who was similar to him in many ways.

# About the Author

Mr. Maldonado is an attorney in the Phoenix area that has practiced insurance coverage and employment discrimination law. He is a co-author/editor of Couch on Insurance, a multi-volume treatise on insurance law. Mr. Maldonado is also a contributing author on CAT Claims: Insurance Coverage for Natural and Man-Made Disasters. Mr. Maldonado also wrote the employment chapter for the Arizona Tort Law Handbook. He has contributed to various law reviews and other articles. Now, Mr. Maldonado takes his hand to an area of personal satisfaction -relationships and emotional experiences.

# Bibliography

This is a list of books and short stories written and published by Daniel Maldonado:

The Palace of Winds and Other Short Stories - A collection of poignant short stories addressing romance, failures, intrigues, and beliefs from a male perspective, reflected by a synopsis of selected stories listed below:

Through Thunder and Light - A follow up to the original compilation "The Palace of Winds and Other Short Stories.

From the Streets of Chambers Lane - The intriguing story of the Mendoza family's unexpected loss of their youngest son and sibling, Michael. Dealing with spiritual struggles and disillusionment as well as familial rivalries and quirky social interactions, the novella introduces the reader to each diverse family member's perspective of the tragic event while personalizing their cultural past and fears of the unknown future.

When Dreams Abound: A Return to Chambers Lane - Fatherless, Daniel Mendoza learns from a myriad of male friends and neighbors who come into his life from childhood to adulthood about what it actually means to be a man.

Lightning Source UK Ltd.
Milton Keynes UK
UKHW022320220221
379219UK00012B/1335/J

9 781034 463962